Ateni Samjak

A Novella

Written by: Michael J. Reppas II

From a story originally conceived by
Michael J. Reppas II and Emanuel J. Comino

e·volve

E-volve Publishing, LLC
8004 NW 154th Street #214
Miami, Florida, USA 33016

Dedication

To him who created the myth that Lord Elgin was a savior and to all those who perpetuate that myth, I add this, heretofore untold story into the collective pool of historical accounts of the pillage of the Parthenon. I add it as a counterpoint to the tales of the heroic journeys of the brave and noble Lord Elgin that have been spun for far too long, and as a tribute to all those real heroes who died fighting for their freedom from oppression. What the Greeks have endured at the hands of the Turks *and* the British is not a myth and neither should be the honorable decision of the British Parliament to right this historical wrong and to return, unconditionally, the Parthenon Sculptures to Greece.

Michael

This powerful work speaks across the generations, reminding us that the voice of Ancient Greece is still with us, infusing and shaping so much of the modern world and inspiring us to this day. This fictional work allows us to understand the trials and deprivations endured by those who sought to protect and conserve Hellenic culture and the Orthodox Faith under a brutal occupation. Elgin's opportunistic looting and vandalizing of the Parthenon and its sculptures during the Turkish occupation, will go down as one of the greatest crimes of history. The wrongs of the past are often difficult to undo, the Parthenon Marbles, must be returned home to Greece.

Emanuel

TIMELINE OF SIGNIFICANT EVENTS

———————— ❧ ————————

431 BC	Parthenon erected in Athens
1453 AD	Fall of Constantinople
	Turkish occupation of Greece begins
1800 AD	British Lord Elgin arrives in Greece
1803 AD	The events of this story take place
1816 AD	Elgin sells Parthenon Sculptures to Parliament
1817 AD	"Elgin Marbles" go on display at British Museum
1821 AD	Greek War of Independence begins

ONE

Trudging up the steps of the British Museum, the old man in the tweed coat and rust-colored cap held the young boy's hand tightly. The boy wanted to skip up the steps, but his Papou George could not keep up with such a pace. His seventy-five years weighed heavily on him, as did the thought of what they would see inside.

The journey he was embarking upon with his grandson this morning was one he had prepared for in mind, body and spirit. It was a lesson in life, history, culture and morality that he was passing on to his last living heir. All the details of how he would accomplish this task were critical as he had to both educate and inspire.

It was more than simply a passing of the torch from one generation to the next. His was an *obligation*. A centuries-old mission that he had vowed to pass on when he first learned the truth from his father so many decades ago. He allowed a tear to fall from his wrinkled eye as he thought of his lost son. He wished it were his son who was instructing the boy with his energetic charm and passion, rather than himself. But that was what fate had decreed. And so, with a mix of ethnic pride, embarrassment, pain and anger all pulling on his soul, much as the boy pulled on his hand, he climbed up the polished steps leading to the giant sized doors of the museum's entrance way.

"Tell me again what we're going to see. Tell me!" little Kostantine insisted.

"The glory of Greece... despoiled," said the old man coldly.

"What does that mean?" asked the boy. *Despoiled* was not in the eight-year-old's vocabulary. The boy's usual toothy grin was replaced by a puzzled frown as he tried to make sense of the unfamiliar words. He stopped between steps and turned to his grandfather for an explanation.

The older man paused momentarily to try to find a way to explain such a complex concept to an eight-year-old, but he soon abandoned the effort, opting for a simple: "It's complicated" response. "We're going to see the Parthenon. I'll explain more to you when we get inside."

The boy knew that the Parthenon was in Athens, not London, but he shrugged his shoulders and accepted his grandfather's words. "Okay, Papou," he said as he surged ahead again, pulling at his grandfather's arm impatiently. At the entrance, little Kosta, full of self-importance at his knowledge of their destination, told the guard at the door, "We're here to see the Parthenon."

"The what? Oh—you mean the *Elgin* Marbles. They're in the Duveen Gallery. That way." He pointed helpfully and smiled a plastic, automatic smile.

"That's not where they belong," George muttered, his voice laced with a heavy Greek accent.

"Pardon me?" asked the employee. "Can I help you?"

"I wish you could," the old man said with a sigh as he led the boy through.

"What's the matter, Papou?" asked Kosta.

George tugged the little boy's hand, urging him inside. He didn't answer the question, though.

The pair made their way through the museum slowly. The boy was impatient, jiggling and wiggling, surging ahead, and doing what looked nearly like a dance step. The grandfather, in contrast, was slowed by age and walked with a noticeable limp. His hair had long since passed from grey to white, even though it was still plentiful. The little boy, dressed in his best suit, had brown hair, a long, thin nose, and serious eyes that made him look far too wise for his eight years.

When George stopped for a moment to look around him, Kosta tugged impatiently at his jacket. "This way, Papou," he said, trying to pull the old man in the direction the guard at the front door had indicated. "Come on!"

George sighed heavily and resumed trudging across the museum. "Don't you want to see the Parthenon marbles?" little Kosta asked as he pulled him onward. "I thought you wanted to see them."

"I do, I do, but not here, my child. Not here."

"But I thought they were here?" questioned the boy in a high, sweet voice.

"They are, and that's the trouble," muttered George to the utter befuddlement of the boy.

They resumed their progress, and George struggled to keep up with the boy's pace.

When at last they reached the Duveen Gallery, Kosta, who was bright for his age and could read well, sounded out the sign. *"El...jin,"* he said. The old man noted that he mispronounced "Elgin" without its intended hard *G,* but the correction that came from his lips, however, was not directed toward his mispronunciation. "They're not the *Elgin* Marbles. They're the *Parthenon* Marbles!" he said authoritatively.

Taken a bit aback, the boy quickly responded. "Don't be mad at me, Papou. That's what the sign said. Look!" he said as he pointed to the sign on the wall. "Maybe we're in the wrong place. Maybe what you are looking for is somewhere else."

The old man's voice softened. "I'm not mad at you, little Kosta, light of my life. I'm mad at *them*. What I want is to see them where they belong."

"Where do they belong, Papou?" Kosta asked earnestly.

The old man stooped down toward the boy with difficulty and put one hand on each shoulder. "On the Parthenon, boy, on the Parthenon. They belong in Athens on the Parthenon... and don't you ever forget it."

"The Parthenon? The building on our calendar at home?"

The calendar the boy was referring to, hung on the wall of the family's kitchen and featured a splendid image of the Parthenon—complete with the marble ornamentation that had been removed from it two centuries earlier.

"The same, my boy, the very same Parthenon. The sculptures that are displayed here in this museum, belong on the Parthenon—and nowhere else. They certainly do not belong here. They were stolen my boy!"

"Can't we call the police?"

The grandfather chuckled a bit before responding. "It is not that simple, my boy. Besides, the crime took place around 200 years ago."

"Two hundred years ago? Then the bad guy who did it is dead?"

"Yes. A long time dead."

"So why doesn't this museum give the pieces back to...well, who *do* they belong to, anyhow? Who did the bad guy steal them from?"

"From the Greek people, my little Kosta, from the entire country of Greece, from the Parthenon itself, from our forefathers, from me and from you." he said without pause.

This was obviously a bit much for the boy, but he must have understood a part of what was explained to him because his next question was simply: "Why won't the museum give them back?"

To that, his grandfather paused and looked at the boy. There were so many different ways to answer this question. Before he could respond, however, the boy continued.

"It isn't right to keep what isn't yours. That's what Mama always tells me."

"You are so right, child. You are so right."

"So they have to give them back. *And there will be no more discussion about it!*" the boy said. The latter part of his statement being accompanied by a shake of his finger toward his grandfather – an inside joke between them referring to how the boy's mother sometimes scolded him when he challenged her too much.

"Yes, yes. Just like your Mama says," the old man laughed. But his smile disappeared a moment thereafter as he caught the boys gaze and stated in an unwaivering tone. "They *have* to be returned to Greece."

The boy nodded before asking his next question. "So who was the bad guy who stole them to begin with?"

"That would be Lord Elgin."

"*Lord* Elgin?" the boy asked.

"That was his title. And that is why some people call them the *Elgin* Marbles. *We* call them the *Parthenon Sculptures*. But they are one and the same." He paused as he let that sink in with the boy.

"The way in which people refer to the sculptures is how you can tell whether they believe they should stay here in this British Museum or whether they believe they should be returned to Greece," he explained.

"Referring to them as the *Elgin Marbles* sends the message that you believe they were the property of Elgin and belong here in this giant trophy case. *We* call them the *Parthenon Sculptures,* because they belong to and are an immovable part of the Parthenon," he said decidedly.

"Let me tell you the real truth of what happened so long ago that resulted in these Sculptures finding their way here so far from home," he continued.

"Is this going to be one of your stories?" the boy interrupted, full of excitement. "I love it when you make up stories, Papou. Tell me a story about the Elgin Marbles... I mean the *Parthenon Sculptures*," he corrected.

The old man took hold of his hand and lowered his face to eye level with the boy. "They say that myths are created to explain the unknown. But myths are also made up to take people away from the known truth," he said with care. "So I will tell you a story about the Marbles, but it will not be a myth, and it will not be one that you have heard before. In fact, you will be one of the very few living people on this earth to know this story... this history." He smiled as he continued with just enough pause to take in his next breath.

"It is a story that has been kept from the archives of history, waiting for you, to hear it. It is a story about a family. A story about oppression. About struggle and sacrifice. About standing up for what is right, no matter the cost. A story of love and hate, of goodness and greed...."

Before he could continue, the young boy interrupted him by raising his hand as if to ask a question of his teacher. "Papou?" he asked. The old man paused, taken a bit off guard by the break in his speech. "Yes, boy?" he finally responded.

"Can you just get on with the story?"

With a quiet chuckle and slight smile he responded. "Of course, boy. Of course. But not just yet. Let us look at the Sculptures now while we are here. I will begin the story later, when we get back to the hotel."

"I want to hear it now, Papou. I want to hear it now!"

"I will tell you when we get to the hotel, my little Kosta... *and there will be no more discussion about it,"* he said, shaking his finger at the boy in furtherance of their joke.

They briefly laughed and then both turned serious as they walked into the gallery.

The story the old man would share with the boy needed an introduction from the sculptures they were about to view.

TWO

The year was 1803. Before cars, or electricity, or telephones, let alone all electronic devices. It was a time when Greece was living a nightmare under the occupation of the Turks. A time when they were slaves.

It was a dark night in Athens and the candles cast a soft glow on the kitchen table, where Irini Politis was setting the cups, plates and utensils down with the help of her daughter, Anastasia. Irini was a natural beauty, with a thin face and body, long black hair and rich, dark eyes. She had a deep, ugly scar over the left side of her face that drew all eyes to it and away from her otherwise flawless beauty. It started just at the corner of her left eye and carried down across her cheek, slightly down her neck. It had healed over time, but it was clear that at one point it must have been a life-threatening accident that caused it.

Irini was in her early twenties and maintained quite an athletic build, in spite of the fact that there were no sports of any kind played in her village by women... or men. In another life she would have been a powerful swimmer or long distance runner, but that was not the life she had. Her's was one of work and of care for her husband, parents, and the beautiful girl before her... too beautiful, perhaps.

As the child helped her mother set plates on the table she couldn't hide her excitement as she looked forward to her father's return from work. Not only because she adored him and he her, but also because he usually had a treat with him when he came home from the bakery. Her father frequently teased her by telling her that she loved her sweets more than she loved him.

"That's not true, Baba! You know it's not!" she would protest, always with her right hand on her hip, her lower jaw jutting out, and her eyes blazing with a playful challenge.

"I know, my sweet, *agapi mou*, I know," he would invariably respond with a laugh, picking her up in the air and swinging her around.

This event would usually be followed by cries of protest from Irini. "Be careful! She's getting bigger, and heavier. I don't want you dropping her!"

"Baba's as strong as Hercules, Mama!" Anastasia would remonstrate. "He won't drop me."

The child adored her father and she loved it when he held her up and swung her around. Her chubby cheeks glowed, her eyes sparkled, and her dark black hair swirled around her head as her father whirled her through the air, to his wife's unending consternation.

Their problems disappeared in those beautiful moments. Love, God and family maintained them and gave them the strength they needed to live their hard lives.

The Politis family was not well off, economically, in spite of the fact that they owned their own bakery, but they were among the more fortunate Greek Christians they knew. They had a two-room home made of wood and mortar, and maintained a small chicken coop and two goats in their courtyard. They paid their taxes, they worked, they ate, and were allowed to go to church - although no ringing of church bells ever occurred, as they had been banned long ago by the Turks. Those less fortunate than the Politis family, without their own family trade or business, were kept impoverished and allowed to live "free" if they worked a Turkish master's fields. Those without options were sold as slaves and disappeared from the village.

As non-Muslims, "*rayahs*" as they were called, their family was required to pay several types of taxes to the *samjak* and local rulers. One tax was known as the "head-tax," because, *quite literally*, you paid it so that you could keep the head on your shoulders. Another tax was called "*jizya*," and this was a type of poll-tax, another per-person tax, which all non-Muslims paid and for which a receipt was issued. Greeks were required to carry their receipt of payment of the *jizya* with them at all times to prove their compliance – the failure of which resulted in enslavement or death.

The harshest *tax*, however, was that of *paidomazoma*, the "child gathering" tax, which the Sultan imposed by taking a male child from each family for conscription into his elite military division known as the Janissary Corps. Such children were taken from their families, converted to Islam, and brainwashed into becoming the perfect soldiers of the Sultan's army – often returning in adulthood to their own villages as soldiers imposing the rule of Muslim law upon their own families. The *paidomazoma* for beautiful girls, however, was even worse as they were sent to live as sex slaves in the Sultan's harem.

Irini brushed a strand of her hair from her eyes and lightly touched the scar along her face. She paused and looked at her beautiful daughter before her. It sickened her to think of what they might have to do to save her. She exhaled strongly, shook her head, and pushed the thought from her mind. She said a quick prayer to God asking for His protection and returned to work.

They lived in a *samjak* ruled by a wealthy Turk called Samjakby Ahmed Kalil. *Ateni Samjak*, as it was sometimes known (the "Athens Samjak"), was one of six divided sections of Greece, where the once-great city of Athens prospered and where now the Christian minority lived. They were kept separate from the Muslim estates not by walls or other barriers, but by absolute fear of death. For any Christian wandering into a Muslim section of Athens would be attacked immediately not necessarily by Turkish authorities but by any Muslim man who would find them. And if such murder did occur, there would be no punishment for the Muslim man - indeed, he would be praised for maintaining the safety and sovereignty of their land from the infidels.

The Greeks were dominated by their Turkish oppressors. Not only were they prohibited from carrying weapons, riding horses, or from ever leaving their *samjak*, they were severely punished, by whip or sword, for any offense, intended or not, against their Turkish lords. The infidel Greeks were beaten into submission and that way of life was passed on from one generation to the next.

And so the Politis family lived, but there was no mistaking that they were not a free people in a free land.

14

Elefterios Politis was a third generation Athenian whose family had come from Constantinople, now known as "Istanbul," just after the City's fall to the Turks in 1453. At the time, Constantinople was the largest, most advanced and developed city in the world. For that reason it was known by most simply as "*the* City," because there was no equal to compare it to. Although last names were used at that time, when Elefterios' great – great - great grandfather escaped and found his way to Athens, he could not remember his given family name. Instead of killing him, the Turkish guards laughed and gave him entry to *Ateni Samjak* by signing his papers as "Elefterios *Politis*" – translated as "Elefterios from the City."

Elefterios was the son whom every father wanted and every mother prayed to God to protect. He was handsome, intelligent, strong, honest, kind and a proud Christian. He was also very anti-Turk. His brother, Michali, had been abducted by the Sultan's Janissaries long ago, and his heart had ached ever since. He was inspired by the events of the Russian-Turkish war years earlier and fully expected Greek Independence to arrive at any moment. To the Turks he was, in a word, dangerous.

And so Anastasia grew up with a rebellious father, a loving mother, and the careful eyes of her maternal grandparents, in whose house the family lived. Papou Andoni and Yia-yia Anastasia, the young girl's namesake, doted on her. She was their everything. Their hopes and dreams - their escape from the monotony of life under Turkish occupation.

Irini worked in the family bakery, tending the counter with her mother, while Elefterios did the mixing and baking in the back brick ovens. Whenever little Anastasia was there, after her lessons in the church school, both mother and grandmother kept an eye on her as she was an active and boisterous child. Not that she was disobedient, but rather because she was simply a whirlwind of energy and a handful to follow. She was a child who was always busy - always doing something and into something else, curious and aware of things far beyond her years.

Her grandfather enjoyed watching her too when he was home, but that was not often. Papou Andoni was a fisherman, and as a result, he left their home before sunrise and returned late every night, smelling of salt and fish. Like his son-in-law, Irini's father had little use for the Turkish invaders who ruled Greece. They controlled their lives as farmers controlled their cattle, constantly keeping them in check and within permissible bounds.

The Politis family gave one-half of all their baked goods to the Sultan every day when his bookkeepers arrived - just as did Papou Andoni with his fish. Full disclosure and a complete and accurate accounting of every item made, purchased, acquired, sold or bartered was obligatory. Three things were required of the Greeks during this exchange. First, never to question the right of the Sultan to his tithe. Second, never to withhold any information or fail to make a full disclosure of what had been made and sold. And, third, never to look the bookeeper in the eyes for too long. Punishment for a violation of any of these three was immediate and permanent.

If the Greek subjects could follow the laws and orders of their Turkish masters without question, they were allowed to live as independent slaves. The terms of their "*freedom*" were simple: do what you are ordered immediately and without question and you can live. So that is exactly what the Politis family did, along with all the other Greeks living in Athens. They succumbed to the rule and authority imposed upon them. Day after day. Week after week. Until one generation passed to the next and the life of slavery was inherited at birth.

But there was hope in some.

In spite of the occupation, both Elefterios and his father-in-law, as well as the two women of the family, considered themselves lucky in one regard. The Turks allowed them to practice their own religion. Despite the fact that their overlords were Muslim, they did not force Mohammed upon the Greeks, and they allowed them to continue their religious practices without too much interference. Mohammed had, after all, recognized Jesus as a prophet. The Turks ruling over these people, however evil they may have been, were true to Mohammed's word and let the Greeks keep their Christian ways.

The Greeks of the time knew that their survival depended upon their being able to live quietly and unobtrusively. Living as just another Greek. Just another face in the same crowd. No one special. Survival depended upon your never shining too much, or becoming too well known amongst the Turks or even the Greeks. It was safer to be recognized by the Turks as "the baker" or "the fisherman," rather than as a person proud of his name, one who felt he had the right to be called by his name.

And that is how the Politis family had lived for as long as any of them could remember, but that was about to change - although the family did not yet know it - on one calm and seemingly ordinary evening in the late summer of 1803.

###

"Will Baba be home soon?" five-year-old Anastasia asked.

"Soon enough, child... soon enough," Irini told her as she bustled around their small kitchen preparing their evening meal. Irini's parents, who currently were in their bedroom napping, would join them when dinner was ready.

Their evening meals were usually the same - - fresh or salted fish that Papou Andoni had caught that day or the day prior, unsold or extra bread from the bakery that day, dandelions and wild greens boiled with lemon juice and olive oil, and fresh milk from their goats. In a good week they would trade bread and fish for cheese and wine, but usually, the fish, salad, bread and milk was all they had.

As always, Anastasia was bouncing around the house, demanding to know, "Will Baba be home soon? Will he? I'm hungry."

"Yes, daughter, yes. *Shush*... Calm down. You'll break the floor with all your jumping around," Irini said, her cautious words ameliorated by a fond and loving smile.

But when Elefterios finally arrived, his demeanor was not his usual calm and cheer. He bolted through the front door and shut it with a strong push of his hand. He was clearly troubled. He did not even remember his manners and entered without a warm greeting for his wife or child. No hugs and kisses today - he was rushed and agitated. Something was wrong.

"What is it, my love?" asked Irini instantly.

Ignoring the disconnect, Anastasia cried out "Baba!" and ran to her father unreservedly. He instinctively caught her as she leapt into his arms, but instead of playing with her, he gave her a quick hug and kiss on the cheek and then put her back on the ground, turning to speak with his wife.

"You know that new English ambassador?" he asked. "The one I told you about last week?" Elefterios ran his hand through his hair, then tugged at his salt-and-pepper moustache. His eyebrows closed ranks as his forehead furrowed.

"Lord Elgin?"

"Yes. That one."

"Baba," interrupted the child, "do you have a treat for me?"

He looked at her with confusion for a moment as if she were speaking another languague, then, realizing what she wanted, he quickly answered: "No, not today, I didn't have time today."

Elefterios quickly tuned back to Irini. "I just heard that *Lord Elgin* intends to tear down the sculptures from the Parthenon and send them to his home in Scotland – to make it pretty for his wife! There is some talk that he has the consent of the Turkish Governor here in Athens, and further talk that he has the written permission of the Sultan himself – which I highly doubt! All the talk in town is that he intends to begin tearing down our Parthenon next week! He is hiring every able-bodied peasant he can find to join his crew and he is paying them, and their Turkish masters, absurd amounts of money to do his bidding. His men have already started passing out food and rum and are walking around the Acropolis like they own it. The people are fighting each other to be first in line to join. Can you believe all of this Irini?" he rhetorically asked.

"It's bad enough that these Turks took over our country and rule it as they do, but now they are allowing themselves to be paid off by this British *lord* to help him steal away our ancestral heritage! This is unacceptable, Irini. They are going too far. That Parthenon is *our* history and they can't give it away. It has to stay where it is! That Parthenon is a marker of our golden past and a reminder to us of what our glorious future may be. We can recapture the glory of our ancestors! We have to keep that inspiration alive for ourselves and our children! We have to do something Irini. *I* have to do something!" he adamantly concluded.

Irini was wide-eyed and aghast. "I don't know what is going on, but I do know that I won't hear of you turning into some kind of rebel. They'll just as soon as kill you as let you challenge them," she reminded him.

Elefterios banged on the kitchen table with a closed fist in frustration.

Irini continued, "My love, what can you do without risking your life and ours?"

There was a slight pause before he responded. "I don't know, but I mean to do something. I will not just stand idly by while this Englishman steals our past. We are still Greeks, after all. We still exist! We are not dead yet, and we cannot allow the vultures to eat our bodies while we still breathe!"

"Hush! Hush!" Irini quietly interjected, "remember that up until now we have survived by getting along with the Turks.. by going along *with* them, not *against* them. And because we have stayed out of trouble and followed their rules, we have been allowed to live our lives without much interference. We are poor, but at least we are alive. At least our family goes onto another generation." She decided to call him by his familiar name "Lefteri" now, rather than his proper name "Elefterios," to play on his affections.

"Lefteri... would you risk all that? Would you risk *us* ?"

"Irini, every day it's a struggle for me to stay a quiet slave to my Turkish masters. It eats me from the inside out to see our glorious Greece under the thumb of these wretched barbarians. I have quietly prayed for the day when we free ourselves from their domination. And now that they are selling our ancient treasures, all we have left, to other slave owners, I have come to realize that I cannot wait quietly any longer."

"But, Lefteri, why? The Parthenon is glorious, yes, but you have never even been permitted to see it up close. They have never let you into the Acropolis, and they never will. I heard they converted half of it into a Mosque already and the other half is an armory. What does it matter if they give part or all of it away to the English? We don't control that. We only control our own actions, which, in turn, decide whether we live or die. I am begging you to control your temper and let this go. I don't want you to do something foolish that we will all regret."

"That's too much for you to say to me, Irini. Too much. I don't know with whom to be more angry—the Englishman who would steal our treasure, the Turks who would allow it, or you, who would prevent me from fighting for what little we have left." His voice was angry, but not soaked with hate.

Irini understood that she had gone too far, but she loved her husband and she wanted to protect him... even from himself. She decided to embrace him and ask for his forgiveness, but before she could cross the room, Elefterios spoke.

"I recognize that I am not in a position to stop the Englishman alone. The authority to speak with the Turks is vested in our town representative and the priest, not the baker. But it is good that we work together to stop this pillage." His voice rose as his enthusiasm grew. "And once we unite to stop this... this ... *theft*, then we can rise up against the Turks and break our chains for good!"

"Lefteri, you must not talk like that!" Irini insisted loudly. "I don't want to hear any more about uprisings and rebellions - or, at least, not about you being a part of those things," she concluded.

"Do you like seeing Greece at the mercy of foreign invaders? Invaders who would allow such a thing as the dismantling of the Parthenon? There's no knowing how many sculptures this Lord Elgin will take. One is too many! Enough is enough! We have reached the tipping point. We are at the point of no return."

"You sound like you are plotting a revolution."

"If that is what it comes to, so be it."

"That is too dangerous! I will not hear of it! They will kill you Lefteri! Kill you! I won't have you putting yourself in harm's way. As your wife and the mother of your child, I have something to say in the matter, and what I say is *No !* Most firmly and unequivocally *No !* I do not wish to be a widow. I don't want to raise our child without you. I will not have Anastasia growing up without a father. If you won't think of your own life, think of hers... think of us. Think of what our lives will be like without you. Think of the burden you would leave me to raise her alone."

"Anastasia is no burden. Our daughter is a blessing from the one true Lord."

"Yes she is," agreed Irini, almost apologetically. "I'm sorry," she said softly as she turned her back to the pot of greens on the wood-burning stove, stirring them more vigorously than they required. "All this talk of revolution scares me, Lefteri."

Elefterios sighed and sank back into a chair. "I will forget about revolution—for now." He tempered his promise. "But I cannot sit back and let this Englishman cart off the Parthenon in pieces. We must... *I*... must do *something*. I agree with you, not a battle against the Turks, but at least open a dialogue with them. A well-thought-out and explained rationale that will show them the importance of preserving the temple as it sits."

"I will talk with a few of the elders tonight, and I will have a meeting with the Prokritoi and Father Germanos to get their permission before I go and talk to the Disdar or the Voivode. The Greeks will support me no doubt, and when the Turkish authorities understand what is going on and see that it is not just one lone, crazy individual who is complaining, when they see that *all* of us Greeks are respectfully and peacefully assembled as a cohesive group, I am sure they will listen to us and that I will be able to explain to them why this planned theft must be stopped."

"You will go peacefully? No threats? No troublemaking?" Irini asked earnestly.

"Yes. We will respectfully ask them to listen to us. We will be polite and sincere." Elefterios stroked his beard and walked around the room, lost in thought. "Perhaps they do not understand the importance, the *significance* of the Parthenon. Perhaps they are so ignorant that they cannot comprehend what the Parthenon is for us; what it means to us. We will go and talk to them. We will explain it to them. We will try to make them see things our way. We will not fight. We will not argue. We will persuade. We will use logic. Okay, Irini, now let me see which of my friends will go with me."

Anastasia sat silently through all of this. Never had she heard her Baba speak with so much passion, so much fire, about anything. At five, she was certainly too young to understand much of what was going on, but she could hear that her father was angry and concerned. As for her mother, she was clearly upset and afraid, and that made Anastasia afraid too, although she didn't know what exactly she was supposed to be afraid of.

The child slipped her hand into her mother's trembling hand and looked up at her face. Irini grasped her daughter's hand reflexively but barely noticed her stare. She knew her child was looking up at her, but her sole focus was on her husband. "What will you do if they say no? If they will not listen to you?" she asked as if pleading with him.

"They will listen," Elefterios replied with a firm voice. Too agitated to sit still, he got up again and began to pace the kitchen, jamming his hands in his pocket only to pull them out again and pound one fist into the other palm. "They will *have* to listen!" he thundered, filled with righteous conviction. "We will have our most persuasive man speak for us."

She was unable to hold back her fear or her tongue, in spite of her previous promise. "Please don't do this, Lefteri. I am afraid for you... for us."

Elefterios responded in a loud and commanding voice. "We are not dogs, Irini. Or slaves. We are a proud people with a rich history. A history that deserves protection. And if we don't step up to protect it, who will? It is my obligation... to my father, my grandfather, to *all* my ancestors. It is my obligation to you and to our daughter, and to her children and theirs. I can not sit back and watch the English steal our past. The Parthenon and all her sculptures belong in Athens and *only* in Athens!"

Irini turned from the stove and simply stared at Elefterios for a long moment before she spoke. "You make our ancestors proud, you make your family proud, you make me proud. And I love you!" Irini slipped an arm around his waist as he paced past her, and he momentarily stopped as he bent his tall frame to his much shorter wife and planted a kiss on her nose.

"Your friends will nominate you to lead the *persuading*," Irini continued. "Just wait. You will see." Then she paused for a moment, "but what if your questions anger the Voivode or the Disdar?"

Anastasia piped up then. "What is a Voivode and dis... that other thing you said?"

Elefterios bent to his daughter, put his hands on her waist, lifted her high into the air, and then brought her chest-to-chest with himself. Slipping one arm under her rump to support her, he held her tightly around her shoulders with his other hand. Her face was very close to his. "You ask a lot of questions," he said with a fond smile. "They are good questions. Someday I bet you will be the smartest girl in Athens."

"You didn't answer my question, Baba."

"I was *going* to." There was a mild reproach in Elefterio's tone. "Have patience, little one. The Voivode is the governor of the city of Athens, and the Disdar is the governor of the Acropolis."

"What is a governor?"

"I see I have to take a step back and start at the beginning. A governor is an official for the government who is in charge of a certain area. He sees to it that the laws are followed in that area, and sometimes he makes the laws himself."

"So, since we live in Athens, this Voivode is in charge of us? Like you and Mama are in charge of me?"

"Unfortunately," sighed Elefterios.

"You would like it if nobody was in charge of us?" the little girl asked. "I know sometimes I wish I didn't have anyone telling me what to do," she said, coyly looking up at her mother.

"Somebody has to be in charge of every city in every country. Otherwise it would be total chaos," her father replied.

"What is chaos?"

"It means that things would be a mess. But the Voivode and the Disdar should not be the people in charge of us."

"Why not? Do they make things more of a mess? You and Mama are good at being in charge of me. So is Yia-yia. So is Papou."

"Thank you, sweetie," said Irini, reaching out to pat the child's leg as it dangled down while her father continued to hold her. Then she returned her attention to what she was cooking while listening to see how her husband would answer the little girl's question.

"The problem, sweetness, is that the Voivode and the Disdar are Turks. They are not Greeks – and they should not rule us."

"Are Turks bad people?"

Elefterios paused to think through a reasoned response before answering her. At last, in measured words, he said, "I am sure that their friends and their countrymen— that is, the other Turks—don't think so, and I am sure their children love them just as you love me and Mama."

"And Yia-yia and Papou," the child cut in.

"Yes, yes," said Elefterios impatiently. "But they are Turks and we are Greeks. They invaded our country. They make the laws and force us to follow them. We are not free," he emphatically stated.

Anastasia drew a deep breath, and Elefterios knew what was coming. Before the child could cut in to ask what "invaded" meant, Elefterios went on to explain.

"Many years ago, the Turkish army poured into our country like a flood of demons and started a war. They killed our leaders, our soldiers, and thousands and thousands of innocent people, until they won the war. Then they took control of our cities and made themselves our rulers. But they have no right to rule us. They are not of our people, they are from a different land and follow a different god." He paused and took a deep breath before he continued.

"It is wrong that they invaded Greece. It is wrong that they made themselves our masters. It is a crime against man and God that they control us and tell us what we can and can not do!" Elefterios, stood from the table and walked toward the kitchen window to collect his thoughts before he continued. Both Anastasia and Irini sat quietly, waiting for him to go on.

"When will this end? When will we be free?" he asked angrily as he turned abruptly to face them.

Anastasia became visibly upset and uncomfortable, and Irini decided to step in to try to calm him. "Elefterios! *Hush*! Calm down!" She put a calming hand on her husband's arm, but he wrenched it free and moved away.

"How can I be *calm* when these—these—these *Barbarians* have taken over our homeland and now are letting *other* Barbarians desecrate our most valuable possessions —our souls, our spirits, our past and our future, our... everything." He sputtered to a stop, too angry and upset to continue.

Anastasia shrank back. She had never seen her father this angry or upset. It frightened her. "Baba, what are you going to do?" she asked.

"Yes," echoed Irini in a tightly constrained voice. "What *are* you going to do?"

"I'm going to go see some of my friends and talk to them about visiting the Disdar and the Voivode."

"I still think that it's dangerous," Irini quietly stated.

"We can not sit back and do nothing. Fate controls us, not the Turks. This is too much for me Irini. I can not live like a slave." Elefterios' jaw was set with determination. He whirled around, facing the door, and reached for his hat.

"You're not going *now* are you? The evening meal is nearly ready," Irini replied. She hoped that filling him with food would quell his sense of urgency.

"You four eat without me. I'm too upset to eat anyhow. Let me go and talk to my friends and see who I can round up to join me. There is strength in numbers."

"Be careful!" she cautioned him. He blew them kisses and dashed away.

After a moment, the young girl turned to her mother. "Why is he so upset about the Parthenon, Mama?" Anastasia's eyes were wide with a mixture of puzzlement and concern. "Did he build it?"

"No, my sweet," she said with a heavy sigh. "Let me check on our supper and then I'll tell you about the Parthenon."

"I'm hungry, Mama. How soon can we eat?" the child asked.

"Soon, child, soon," Irini replied.

"Are we going to wait for Baba to get back?"

"Have a piece of bread to hold you over. Supper will be ready soon, don't worry." Irini went into the kitchen, stirred the pot of greens, and made sure they weren't burning or sticking to the bottom of the pot. She lowered the flame just a little and then broke off a chunk of bread for her daughter. The little girl walked over to her mother and put her hand out for the bread, but the mother wagged her finger at Anastasia reprovingly. "Sit down at the table here, so you don't get crumbs on the floor."

Anastasia sat and turned to face her mother as she took a big bite of the bread, freshly made at the family's bakery that day. "Turn around," her mother reproached her. "Eat over the table."

"Okay, okay… now please tell me about the Parthenon," she implored.

"Please don't talk with your mouth full. Honestly, where are your manners?" Irini took the sting out of her words, however, by fondly rumpling her daughter's long, wavy, dark brown hair as she walked past her. Then she sat down at the table and looked at the girl. Irini's eyes were blank, though. She wasn't seeing Anastasia. She was seeing, in her mind's eye, the soon-to-be-despoiled structure so beloved by all Greeks.

"The Parthenon, *eh* ?" A smile curved her lips. "I wish I had seen it when it was first built. I'm told it was full of beautiful colors then. Ah well…." She partially stood as if to leave.

"Tell me!" her daughter repeated impatiently. "Come on!"

Irini smiled and sat back down. "Okay, okay. The Parthenon is a temple that was built to honor the goddess Athena, who you know all about from all the stories of the mythology your Papou Andoni has told you."

The child nodded, and Irini continued.

"Good. Well, back in the Golden Age, amazing temples were built by our ancestors as a sign of thanks, as a form of worship and as a way of honoring the Twelve gods, like the ancient goddess Athena."

"Ancient?" the girl asked, confused by the word.

"That means old."

"She was an old lady?"

"No," Irini said with a laugh. "The Parthenon was built in ancient times. A long time ago."

"How long ago?"

"They say that the Parthenon has stood for more than two thousand years."

"Is that before Jesus was born?" the child asked.

"Yes it is, in fact," her mother replied.

"Wow. That was a long time ago."

"Yes. Isn't it incredible that it is still standing today?"

"I guess. Who built it?"

"A large group of people deserve credit for building the temple, not just one person," Irini stated.

"There were too many, more than I know, involved, but some of the most famous people involved were General Pericles, Phidias – the sculptor, and Iktinos and Calicrates – the architects. General Pericles had just led the Athenians on one of the most important victories against the Ottoman Turks that had ever taken place. His Athenian forces saved all of Greece from the onslaught of the Barbarian Turks... they called themselves *Persians* back then. It was because of his incredible leadership and skills that Athens, Greece, and probably every other land to the west, remained free." She paused as she thought of her life today and the irony of the Turkish occupation over her and all the other Athenians. "Oh, that he were alive today...." Anastasia said nothing, but continued to watch her mother and listen intently to her every word.

"General Pericles was a hero in Athens at the time, a champion, another Hercules. The people all loved him, the government supported him and with this good fortune, he decided to have the Parthenon built, or should I say 're-built,' to stand as the greatest temple in all the world, to honor the goddess Athena for her care and protection over the Athenians, and to serve as a symbol of the greatness of the Greeks and of the divine right they had to live free." As Irini spoke, she realized how much like Lefteri she sounded. She was pleased with herself and her explanation to the child.

"Why did you say 're-built' before?" the child asked.

"Well, the Parthenon that you see today way up on the Acropolis is not the first temple that was built there. General Pericles was insistent on building a new Parthenon there because the Turks had destroyed the one that was there before. Pericles, and the rest of the Athenians, were so disgusted and offended that the Persians would desecrate their glorious and sacred temple, that they used that as a rally cry to motivate the people into fighting against the Turks... and it worked." Irini paused again, as she thought about the irony in this historical fact and the events that were unfolding before them.

"They're doing it again," she thought to herself. "Is history repeating itself?"

As if reading her mind, Anastasia asked "is that why Baba is so mad Mama? Because the Turks are going to destroy the Parthenon again?"

Irini considered her response before speaking. "Yes, my sweet. That is *exactly* why your father is angry."

"You're angry too Mama," the child stated.

"I guess you're right. I am angry too."

There was a catch in Irini's voice, and Anastasia recognized it. Getting up from the table, she walked around to where her mother was seated and said, "Don't cry, Mama. Baba will make it all better. He always does." Her voice was serious, and her thin, small left arm wrapped itself as far around her mother's shoulders as it would go.

Irini acknowledged the fact that her daughter was trying to comfort her, and turned quickly to hug her. "Thank you, honey," she whispered. Then, forcing a smile, she pushed her chair back and got up. "Come on. Dinner must be about ready. Go call Yia-yia and Papou to come to the table."

When her grandmother came to the table and saw the conspicuously empty space in front of Elefterios's place, she raised an eyebrow at Irini. Elefterios was never absent for dinner. The house was small enough, and Elefterios was loud enough, that Irini did not have to explain what had happened. The grandmother's eyes narrowed and she shook her head. "He had best be careful. The Turks don't like seditious talk."

"He is not starting an uprising, Mother," Irini answered with more certainty than she felt. "He is merely trying to organize a group to *petition* the Turks not to let this Englishman destroy our beloved Parthenon."

"All the same—" Irini's father cautioned as he entered the room, "this is a delicate matter... and I'm going to look into it myself."

Papou Andoni was nearly seventy – and looked every day of it. He was still lean and strong, but his burnt skin, calloused hands and deep wrinkles showed his age. What was left of his hair was completely white, although his large, curled moustache still showed a bit of its original black color. His eyes, though, reflected a caged anger, like a domesticated old tiger, who wasn't completed tame. He was the kind of man who always looked hungry, even after he'd just eaten.

Anastasia's grandmother, on the other hand, was in her mid-forties, but she looked surprisingly young. An otherwise plain looking woman, unattractive to most at first glance, the grandmother kept her hair, an obvious affectation of hers, in pristine condition. It was long, straight, and perfectly braided, with a single red strip of cloth acting as the bow. One thin strip of grey interrupted the solid wave of blackness covering her. As part of her evening rituals, she combed her hair one hundred times on each side, making sure that no knots of any kind ever existed, and every morning she took the time to comb it out again and braid it tightly. In her eyes, this made her pretty, and it kept her happy to maintain it.

As far as the grandmother's skin was concerned, her face was tight and slightly tanned. She cared for her skin by cleaning her face twice a day with a mixture of olive juice (which she collected from left over meals) and fish oil (which her husband brought to her every day after he cleaned and gutted his daily catch). Irini, on the other hand, refused to use any such remedies to care for her face; her scar was the only make-up she would ever use.

Yia-yia Anastasia also watched her food intake and limited the amount of breads and pastries she ate – which was no small task considering the daily exposure she had to them at the bakery. Instead, she ate as many nuts, fruits, and vegetables as were available. Tomato, cucumber, onion salads with a small sprinkle of feta cheese were, for her, the best dessert one could ever have.

In these ways, she maintained herself and, not so coincidentally, this was why she looked years younger than she actually was. Indeed, she and her daughter looked more like cousins than parent and child. But that was the real evidence of her age, the fact that she had a twenty-four-year old daughter and a five-year-old-granddaughter.

To an outsider of today's generation, it might appear shocking that they were a married couple with such an apparent age difference between them, but in those days it was common for such age differences to exist between a husband and wife; almost expected. They had been married for close to twenty-five years by this time, and in spite of the hardship of their lives under Turkish rule, they felt blessed to have had such a beautiful daughter and now granddaughter gifted to them by God. They thanked the Lord every day for those blessings, and they included the gift of a good son-in-law in their prayers.

In a house as small as theirs it was virtually impossible to keep secrets from each other. And so as Irini continued watch over their meal, her mother approached the table and took a deep whiff of the aroma emanating from the serving plate and the bowls. "Your husband will be sorry he missed this dinner," she observed.

"All the more for us," Papou Andoni said, rubbing his hands together as he took a seat at the table.

Yia-yia made a swatting motion toward her husband. "We'll leave his portion under the coals to keep warm for when he comes home," she chided him. "Don't you think a man is entitled to some sustenance after a hard day at work?"

"I have been telling you that for years, woman," he said in agreement. "For once it appears as if you have actually been listening to me."

"Thank you, Yia-yia," Irini said to her mother. Since Anastasia's birth, both Irini and her husband had taken to calling Irini's parents "Yia-yia" and "Papou," rather than by their first names, when the child was present in the room.

"*Mmmm, good!*" Papou declared, as he took in a deep breath of the steam pouring from the cooked fish before him.

"What talented fisherman caught these remarkable creatures?" he rhetorically asked as he reached down and grabbed a small fried fish with his bare hands.

"Set a good example!" Anastasia chided him, her eyebrows knit into a frown. "How is our granddaughter to learn manners if she sees you acting like a Barbarian?"

"I was only complimenting the responsible parties," he protested defensively.

"As I am the cook *responsible* for this lovely feast, I thank you for the compliment," Irini said. She couldn't help but add: "but Yia-yia is right. We all need to set a good example, *so no using your hands Papou!*" she said with a mock serious tone that caused the child to laugh.

After their prayers, which included Anastasia's unexpected mention of her father's meeting with Father Germanos, they began to eat. The adults were obviously nervous and concerned over what was going on with Elefterios, but they did not speak of it so as not to concern the child. When the silence went on for a noticeable amount of time, Papou Andoni decided to break the silence with a humorous question and an intentional reaching across the table with his bare hands to grab another piece of fried fish.

"Is there enough for me to have some more?" he asked.

Yia-yia sighed at this latest breach of manners. Anastasia laughed.

"I'd like more too, Mama," Anastasia piped up.

"Clearly you didn't make enough," Papou said with a disappointed tone.

"I made the same as always," Irini protested.

"I guess that your cooking is just particularly good tonight, so naturally everyone wants extra," soothed Yia-yia, playing the peacemaker.

After their meal, Irini cleaned Anastasia, they said her prayers together, and then put her to sleep. The three of them then sat at the kitchen table, quietly waiting for Elefterios to return.

THREE

Konstanine pulled himself up a little higher on his pillow as his grandfather paused to take a sip of his honey-tea. The young boy's eyes were wide with interest in the story. It was already past his bedtime, but since it was a Saturday evening his grandfather would continue with the story until the boy fell asleep.

"How do you like the story so far?" the old man inquired.

"I'm not sure, Papou," he meekly responded. "It's kind of scary. Is it real?"

"Yes boy, the enslavement of the Greek people was very real."

The boy pulled his sheets up a little closer to his neck and contemplated his grandfather's words.

"The sculptures that the little girl's father was talking about are the same one's we saw at the museum, right?" he asked.

"That's right," his grandfather responded.

"Then I know how the story ends."

"No son, you only know how *one part* of the story ends. What you don't know is the rest of the story. There are many museums that are filled with stolen art and artifacts, but the story of those pieces does not *end* at the museum where they are on display in those trophy cases. Son, just because they are in these museums now, today, does not mean that you simply end your interest in their history there. Those pieces were not there *yesterday*, and they may not be there *tomorrow*. Today is not forever. Where they are, where they should be, and where they will be might not be all in the same place. Every piece has its own story and its own destiny – just as you and I do." He took time to make sure that they young boy understood his words and when he received a wordless nod from the boy he continued.

"I understand that this is a lot for you to take in, so I want you to feel free to ask me any questions you have about the story so far. It's important that you understand."

The boy further pushed himself up on his pillow before he asked his next question.

"Why was the mother's face burned?"

The old man paused and took a short breath before answering calmly. "Her face was *cut,* not burned. And that was done because she was very beautiful and her parents were afraid that she would be taken away by the Turks because she was too pretty."

"Why would they do that?" the boy asked.

"The reasons are for someone a lot older than you, but all you need to know at this time is that the Turks often kidnapped beautiful girls and took them away from their families."

The boy thought quickly and responded. "And they took the strong boys for their army, right?"

"That's right," the grandfather responded, glad that an early discussion of the birds and the bees was seemingly avoided. "They took the best Greeks that they *saw* with their eyes, but not necessarily the best Greeks that *were there.*"

The boys eyes furrowed, but before he could ask a follow-up question the old man continued.

"They could see the *outside* of the Greek children, but they could not see the *inside.* They could tell just by looking at them if they were strong or pretty, but they could not know if they were *smart.* They could not judge if they were *intelligent.* And the truth is that the Turks believed that the Greeks were inferior to them intellectually, so all that mattered was what was on the outside.

I understand that this is a difficult concept for you to understand: slavery. You don't know of such things. You don't understand why black people were slaves in America because you were never taught to hate anyone because of the color of their skin or because of their religion. I am sure that you never even knew that our Greek ancestors were slaves at all, did you?" he asked.

"No," the boy responded. "I didn't know that."

"How could you? What you know of Greece does not include such history. You, and virtually all of this generation, are taught only of the glory of ancient Greece, the 'Golden Age' they call it, and of its mythology, nothing else really. And there is much else to teach," he said with a sad exhalation. "Not all of it good, mind you, but none of it that should be forgotten. There was a time when the greatest minds the world had ever known converged in time and space into our homeland. A time when the greatest mathematicians, scientists, philosophers, and artists of every kind lived together, as free men, and collectively brought the world from its intellectual darkness to its first true Renaissance. A time when mankind advanced. When governments became *democratic* – like those in America and Australia. A time when the greatest warriors on land and sea battled the evil empires, *the Barbarians*, and won. But that time came and went. And a dark time followed. A nearly four-hundred-year shadow of darkness was cast over Greece, and the story I am telling you now takes place during that dark time."

The boy pushed himself up on the pillow again as a yawn involuntarily overcame him.

"Perhaps we should end here and pick up in the morning," his grandfather stated.

"No, no Papou. I want you to continue. Please, please continue. Tell me what happened when the Baba got home," the boy asked earnestly.

"Okay, okay," the old man said. "I'll tell you just a little more tonight." He took another sip of his tea and then continued.

FOUR

It was past midnight when Elefterios finally came home - a late hour indeed for someone who was usually in his shop before the crack of dawn. Irini's parents and Anastasia were all asleep in the bedroom, but Irini herself stayed up in the kitchen, reading her worn Bible by candlelight, waiting for her husband to come home.

When she heard the knob of the front door softly rattle, she looked up expectantly. Elefterios was trying to enter quietly so as not to wake anyone, but he had noticed the candlelight on his approach so he knew Irini was waiting for him. Irini quickly rose and went to hug him.

"It's all right," he said comfortingly reassuring her. "No problems. Everything went fine."

"I saved some fish and greens for you. Let me heat it up quickly for you," she said, as she let go of his waist and moved toward the oven.

Elefterios put up a hand to stop her. "I'm too tired to eat," he said. "I just want to get some sleep. This has been a long day."

"You need to eat," she protested.

"I ate a little at Manoli's house. He and his wife insisted. With Father Germanos there, they were obligated to put something out and it would have been rude of me not to eat anything. It wasn't a full meal, but it was enough to hold me over."

Irini then retook her seat at the table and prompted him to join her. "Please tell me about your night —unless you need to go to sleep immediately."

"Tired as I am, I'm still too excited to sleep," Elefterios replied, "and you deserve to hear the full story anyway."

"Tell me, then—what did our famous Prokritoi have to say? Did he tell you to be quiet and mind your business?" Irini spoke with a half-sarcastic tone because their official town representative to the Turks, known as the *Prokritoi*, was Elefterios' oldest brother Manolis. Manolis was thirteen years Elefterios' elder, but he acted like he was his father; always telling him what to do and what not to do.

"No Irini. He listened to me. Both he and Father Germanos listened to me. In fact, about half way through my speech, they interrupted me because they wanted to go and get a few other men to come and listen as well. It was..." he paused as the words came to him, "powerful."

Irini straightened her back, not expecting to hear this. She cocked her head and chin a bit, briefly squinting at him as if trying to understand what he had just said.

"So who came?"

"Four men, and they are all in agreement to go with me. It's a start. Not as many as I'd like, but it's a good start. "

"What are you talking about? *You're* not going anywhere, the *Prokritoi* is our representative, *he and the priest* are the ones who are going to talk to the Turks, not you!" her voice rose in anger and defiance at this. "What, are you the leader now?"

Almost instantly she regretted her words. She did not mean to suggest that he was incapable of leadership, but was only trying to keep him away from actually speaking with the Turks. Elefterios understood and did not need an apology or explanation.

Irini shrugged and, in a more peaceful tone, continued. "I am sorry, husband. I am just a little confused here. Can you go a step back and tell me who was there with you?"

"Yianni and Grigori from the fish shop, Giorgos the butcher, and my brother Alexi. So six altogether, not including myself."

"What did you tell them?"

"Just what I told you – that we have to stop this Elgin, that we have to stand up for ourselves and our history, and that we have to reason with the Turks and convince them that they can not allow this man to steal our most prized possession."

"Did they agree?" she asked.

"Manoli, Germanos, Yianni and Alexi - yes. The others did not agree or disagree. They were unwilling to speak up. They are afraid to confront the Turks about anything. So we decided that just the five of us would go and see the Voivode today. We'll convince him."

Irini draped her arm over Elefterios' shoulders and squeezed gently. She was still unsure if this all wouldn't lead to a bad end. "Are you sure no harm can come to you as a result of this meeting? I've never heard of someone other than the Prokritoi or a priest having an audience with the Voivode. It seems improper. Are you sure about this?" she asked again.

"Yes I am!" Elefterios got up on his elbow, his voice rising in concert with his body. "I can't imagine any harm will come from a simple discussion, but this *is* something important enough to justify the effort. That is *our* Parthenon that the Englishman wants to steal. We may have no means to physically stop him, but if we beseech the Turks, I am sure that they will rescind any permission given to this lord. I just don't think they understand the importance of what they are giving away. Besides, doing nothing is not a real option, is it?"

"Doing nothing and risking your life are two very different things, Lefteri," she said. "But I won't challenge you any further. I will just support you with my heart, my mind, my soul, and whatever else you want from this scarred body." Irini's reference to her face was not missed by him. Lefteri brushed his hand against her cheek and kissed her warmly. It was what was on the *inside* of her that made him love her, and she had just reminded him of that with her words of support.

"Don't worry, Irini, surely even the heartless Turks will not kill a man for asking them to do what is right. The Koran requires them to do what is right, and they will," he said.

"Yes, but you, *as a Greek*, have no right to tell them anything – they decide and they alone. You will have to approach them with that in mind. Perhaps by using an example of some famous mosque that they prize over all the others? Or maybe use Mecca as an example? How would they feel if one of the Seven Mosques in Mecca were taken to a foreign land? Maybe *that* example will help them understand?" she said in earnest.

"That is an excellent approach. And besides, they let the Parthenon sit for hundreds of years now, so I think a part of them *has* to recognize its significance to us, else they would have destroyed it long ago.

"Exactly," Irini interjected. "They respect it so much that they built their mosque directly into it, as a part of it, rather than tear down any of the Parthenon itself. *That* is respect!" she concluded.

"Right," Elefterios agreed. "So what incentive do they really have for letting him do this? None, I say!" They both nodded in agreement.

"You know," Irini added, "I thought that it is against their law to tear down any mosque, so how can they let this Englishman take any part of the Parthenon down? Wouldn't that require that he also destroy part of the mosque in the process?"

"Perhaps... yes," Elefterios agreed. "And the Sultan would never allow that."

"Right, but then what of your belief that the Turks feel indebted to the English for taking up arms against the French when they took the port at Alexandria? So now, are we witnessing the return of that act? The English helped the Turks against the French, so now the Turks feel they owe the English a favor, *and we Greeks are the ones to pay the price.*" Irini's voice raised in anger.

"I think you understand politics much better than I do, because what you explain seems plausible and correct, my dear." Elefterios kissed the top of his wife's head. "For a woman, you are very wise." He meant no disrespect to his wife - he meant only to compliment her reasoning and analysis. Irini was indeed exceptional in many respects, not the least of which was her intelligence and understanding of what went on in the world around her.

Irini also understood—perhaps better than her husband—the danger in opposing the Barbarians who ruled over Greece. Although not normally hot-headed, Elefterios was impassioned in his love of his native land, its history, and its culture. Irini, too, was horrified at the prospect of Lord Elgin dismantling any part of the Parthenon, but she valued her life, her security, and that of her family over the future of the Parthenon. The Parthenon, after all, was just a building. Her husband and the rest of her family were flesh and blood, far more significant to her than *any* building.

"Without Greeks, what value does ancient Greece really have?" she thought to herself.

Irini slowly rose and began to pace across the floor in their small kitchen. Elefterios watched her without saying a word. He knew she was focused on an issue, and he sat patiently waiting for her bring him into her internal conversation. She continued to pace for a long minute before she was ready to continue.

"Lefteri, my dear husband. The path you are taking is a dangerous one. Even Saint Philothei, the reverent and worshipful nun from our very town, was cruelly beaten and killed by the Turks for challenging their laws. A nun, Lefteri, a woman of God who lived in a monastery. They beat her and left her for dead in the streets," she coldly said.

"They killed her because she was buying women slaves from Turks and taking them into the monastery, turning them into nuns."

"I know Lefteri. I know *why* they killed her, but I want you to be reminded of the fact that they did, in fact, *kill* her. A small, frail woman was slaughtered, just as *thousands* of our fellow Greeks and our ancestors have been slaughtered by these Barbarians. No one is too important to avoid their fists or swords. They have killed and continue to kill priests and nuns, the elderly and our children. We are less than humans to them, Lefteri... we are their slaves." She paused as this set in both of their minds. Elefterios understood her point and was reminded of the cruelty of their oppressors.

"I fear what you are getting yourself into," she said, trembling as she put her hand on his shoulder. "I fear that you will be martyred for standing up."

"We all will die, Irini. I just don't want to die without ever having lived. I don't want to die as a slave, I want to die as a man. *A free man*. My spirit belongs to Christ. The Turks can have my blood and bones."

Without another word, the two embraced. Irini quietly cried as she took Elefterios hand and led him to the bedroom, where everyone else was sound asleep. They lay in the darkness, both staring up at their black ceiling, lost in thought.

FIVE

"And with *them* going to sleep, I think we should as well," the old man quietly announced to the boy.

"No, please... just a few more minutes," the boy half-protested.

"We'll pick up in the morning with the Politis family when they wake up as well."

The old man pulled the boys sheets up to his neck, softly patted him on the head, and wished him a goodnight. The boy did not protest further, and he rolled over and almost immediately fell asleep.

The old man turned on a lamp adjacent to the boy's bed and slowly left the bedroom - quietly closing the door behind him. He took a cold bottle of water from the mini-fridge, pulled the footstool next to the large chair across from the television set, and sat down, exhausted. He was too old for this, he thought to himself. He opened the water bottle, took a large sip, and exhaled with satisfaction. He removed his shoes, pulled his tired legs up to the footstool and finally relaxed.

He closed his eyes momentarily, and his subconscious mind was rewarded by the visage of a young man smiling at him with loving eyes. "Michael... Michael," he called out as his hands stretched out to hold him. "I miss you my boy, I miss you" he whispered as tears began to pour from his eyes. "I miss you so much...." He cried softly for several minutes while images and memories of his son came and went from his mind's eye.

The wound was still not healed for the old man. It would never be healed. His conscious mind fought with his subconscious in an effort to reject the joyous link between father and son. It hurt him too much. Forcing his conscious mind to reclaim his senses, the old man shook his head and returned to the physical world.

He wiped the tears from his eyes with the back of his hands and took another sip from the water bottle. He exhaled deeply, realizing that he was even more exhausted than before. His body, his mind, and his spirit were so tired, but he knew he had more yet to do before he could finally rest.

He closed his eyes and said a quiet prayer. "God, give me the strength to pass this torch once more. Please dear Lord, give me just enough days to make sure that the story is not lost. Let me do this to fulfill my son's obligation and, indeed, my own. Let me do so because it is right... and the truth... and what *justice* requires. Thank you, dear Lord, for your blessings and strength. Kiss my son next to you now and remind him of my love. Protect him as I will try to protect his son here on earth. In your name I pray. Amen."

The old man was now calm and relaxed. Sleep came quickly to him. Finally, he was rewarded with a bit of peace.

SIX

On a normal day, Elefterios would precede Irini to the bakery by several hours. He would begin his work day by emptying the jars full of raisins and water that were fermenting on the pantry shelves. Elefterios carefully spooned the raisins from the bottom of each jar and discarded them. The water, which had fermented with the raisins over the last two days, created a natural yeast that he poured in a precise amount to his first mix. He then went to a large bin under his baking table which was full of freshly pounded wheat flour and scooped up several shovels-full of same, adding each to the mix. Elefterios never used any measuring cups to gage the amount needed, everything was done from memory and that baking instinct that some people simply have.

Each loaf was sold by its weight. The smallest, the half kilo, was the most popular and, accordingly, the one that Elefterios prepared the most of. Although most bakers had a variation of wheat and raisin bread, he knew that his was the best, and Elefterios took much pride in the quality of this bread in particular.

He stirred the mixture for several minutes until he was satisfied with the consistency. He then added several scoops of raisins from another covered bin and stirred them in carefully. A few minutes later, he began the process of pulling out clumps of the sticky mixture and rolling that dough into the oblong shape of the bread he was preparing.

Without pause he rolled out dozens of loaves and placed them side by side on the countertop – covering them with a warm, damp cheesecloth as he continued. When the batch was complete, he turned his attention to cleaning the pot, giving the bread the time it needed to rise. There was no rush for him to get the bread to rise, because he knew more or less when it would be ready, but how long exactly it took was up to the bread, not Elefterios. He was patient and busy with other work in the meantime.

After the pot was clean, he turned his attention to the oven and began igniting the coals and wood in the hearth. He carefully stoked the flames to ensure that the oven reached the exact temperature needed to properly bake the breads.

"Everything in its own time," he thought to himself as he watched the flames slowly rise. When the temperature was to his satisfaction, he slid the loaves into the oven with his *fournofiaro*, the long-handled baker's tool with a flat paddle on the end.

Group by group, he would bake and remove the breads, until his first batch was complete. Once all the loaves from the first batch were dusted with flour and placed in their selling shelves for Irini, he would turn his attention to the next bread mixture and repeat the earlier dance.

Irini usually arrived at the shop after Elefterios was in the middle of baking his second batch of loaves. She was delayed in arriving, because she always prepared breakfast for Anastasia, herself, and her mother. Papou Andoni was never at the house in the morning, as he left in the early dawn hours, hoping for a good catch and a cool breeze.

On this day, as with all others, Irini saw to it that Anastasia was properly dressed and ready to spend the day under her grandmother's supervision. First at church for her reading, history and religious lessons with Father Germanos, and then to the bakery. After grandmother and daughter were off, she would lock up their home and head down the narrow streets to the bakery. Invariably she would smell the baking bread well before she arrived at the shop. The delightful smell seemed to curl its way down the street, pulling passers-by into the shop almost involuntarily. Irini, like so many others, loved to follow her nose there every morning.

Once at the shop, however, it was work that awaited her, not a scrumptious treat. After she greeted her husband, she would put on an apron and tend to the customers from behind the counter. Often times there was a small line of people waiting for her to open the front door. Her work began the instant she arrived, and she paused only if the Pasha's accountant came by to check their output and sales logs, and to collect the *jizya*.

Invariably, after he took his portion of their funds from her wooden cash box, he would smile and politely take an armload of fresh bread from the shelves for himself. Irini would always pretend not to notice this act and never said a word about the theft. She certainly never looked the man in his eyes when he was stealing in front of her. She had to let it go. It was just part of their life, something they simply had to accept.

Elefterios spent the entire day in back of the shop by the hot, stone oven. Mixing, cleaning, tending to the fire and monitoring the progress of his baked goods in the oven. It was a hard and busy life, but because of the quality of his product, it was one he was very proud of and enjoyed. Regardless of the circumstances, he was an exceptional baker, and that gave him a sense of pride.

In the late afternoon, after the last of the baked goods were out of the oven and placed on the shelves for sale, Elefterios would come to the front of the shop to join his wife behind the counter. He would relax for a bit then, have a coffee and smoke from his *aryilé*, the tobacco water pipe or "*hooka*," as the Turks called it. An hour or so after that, they would both close up and return home together.

If it were a religious holiday or a special day for one of their immediate family members, they would use the bakery oven to prepare their evening meal, usually mutton or roasted lamb. Otherwise, they would take home with them whatever unsold loaves of bread remained from the day to accompany their fish and greens evening meal. Although they did not have much opportunity to talk during the day, they still enjoyed the thought that they were working together. It was comforting for one to know where the other was... to know that the other was safe.

On this particular morning, however, Irini smelled no warm bread on her way into the shop, and this worried her. She found herself rushing down the street, worried as to what the problem was with Elefterios, praying between huffs that he was fine. When she arrived, instead of finding him working in the back oven, she found him at the front counter, talking quietly to his friend Yianni. She remembered that Yianni was one of the men whom Elefterios had named the night before as wanting to accompany them on their talk with the Voivode.

Yianni stopped talking abruptly when Irini entered the store and his face went stone blank, completely expressionless.

"It's all right, Yianni... Irini knows all about it," Elefterios said, laying a hand on Yianni's arm. Irini detected a note of pride in her husband's voice, which made her happy. She was relieved that he was fine, but part of her was also concerned as to how far behind they were in making their breads for the day.

Irini knew he was proud of her intelligence and wisdom, and at that time in history, such pride from a husband toward his wife was a gift from God, in her mind. While most Greek wives contented themselves with managing their households and raising their children, Elefterios' wife had knowledge and character... substance. She wanted to work with him, to assist him, to make his work *her* work, to participate and contribute.

Instead of feeling threatened or emasculated by this, Elefterios, unlike his counterparts, felt that her *gifts* were traits to encourage rather than to fear or oppress. Besides, there was enough oppression in their lives. "If God willed her to be intelligent and driven, then who am I to oppose it," he often said. "My role is to water His seed."

Turning to Irini now, Elefterios quickly brought her current with his and Yianni's conversation. The men were talking of recent developments regarding Elgin and his efforts at removing the sculptures from the Parthenon.

There were several rumors floating about, but, apparently, Elgin's men had removed one of the *metopes*, a very large figure it was said, and they were building a crate to box it up and send it away.

44

"Gregori's cousin, Filipos, overheard some of the Voivode's men talking about it yesterday," Yianni told Irini. "They apparently thought that Elgin's men were just going to make some kind of copy of the temple with some mortar, or just have some artists draw and paint it. Even the Turkish guards, *Allah take them*, seemed shocked that any part of the temple was actually being removed."

Irini quickly turned to Elefterios and asked, "I thought you said that Elgin had some kind of written permission from the Sultan?"

He nodded in agreement.

"You have to ask for a copy of that...," she began before she paused, "but how can you do that without getting your head chopped off just for asking?" Her question carried on as the three of them contemplated more.

"Regardless of what the written permit says," Irini began before Elefterios interrupted her.

"*If* there is any written permit," he corrected.

"Right," she agreed. "Regardless, it is clear that the Turks are allowing him to act."

"Even with their mosque being there?" Yianni asked.

"Apparently so," Irini replied. "So we need to figure out *why* and then we can try to figure our the best way to stop him."

"Perhaps it is because of what you suggested yesterday, Irini," Elefterios said. "The Turks feel indebted to England for siding with them against the French."

"Perhaps," Irini replied, "but there is likely more to it than that."

Elefterios nodded in agreement. "We have a lot of questions that need answering," he said, "but I am already far behind in my preparations for the shop. Irini, I am just going to have time to prepare two batches of loaves today, so let me get at it, and you can go home early when you sell them. Tell everyone that I am sick so we don't have any accusations that we sold bread that we are not properly accounting for to avoid the *jizya*. I'll come straight home after the meeting and will give you all the details then," he concluded.

"When, exactly, are you intending to meet with the Disdar?" she inquired.

"Father Germanos said the best time would probably be after their second prayer, the *Dhuhr* prayer, in the afternoon."

"Excellent, then" Yianni interjected. "I am certain we will be successful." He sounded confident as he rose to leave.

"I wish I were so sure," Irini replied.

Elefterios said nothing, but his face mirrored her concern.

SEVEN

As they arrived at the bottom of the Acropolis, the five Greeks formed a single file line and slowly began to approach the Sentry's office. They had agreed on this formation to approach the Turkish authorities to show their organization, and their compliant, non-threatening disposition. They intentionally sought to avoid the gang-like look that might have been misinterpreted by the Turkish guards had they traveled side by side. Especially in light of the fact that they were coming to ask a favor of the Disdar, they wanted to show their respect from the outset.

There were two heavily armed guards at the external gate of the Sentry's office, watching their approach. The Greeks walked slowly, tugging at their clothes and smoothing their hair all the while; wanting to make a good appearance and impression.

In spite of the accepted role of the Prokritoi to speak, the men had nominated Elefterios to be their spokesman because of his great knowledge and appreciation of the Parthenon. They had, accordingly, placed him first in line of their formation. In spite of this, it was Alexi – second in line – who spoke up in his eagerness, excitement, and fear, when they reached the guards.

"We've come to speak to the Disdar," he said matter-of-factly.

The larger of the two brutes approached the men with one hand on the hilt of his sword and an unexpected smile on his face.

"That's nice," he said as he eyed them up and down. "Do you all have an appointment this afternoon?" he politely asked.

46

They were pleasantly shocked by the congeniality of the guard, and their spirits lifted. Alexi continued with a cheerful reply, "Well, we don't actually have an appointment, but…" he began before the guard forcefully interrupted.

"Of course you don't, you Greek dog, so shut up!" he belted out in a harsh tone as he glared at them. At this the second guard placed his hand on the handle of a whip at his side and slowly pulled it out. The joy of the five men disappeared in an instant.

The first guard then ordered them to identify themselves.

The Greeks stood still at attention as the guard approached them, one by one, for an apparent inspection. He stopped in front of Elefterios and lowered his towering head and shoulders until his eyes were level and only inches away from his own.

After quietly clearing his throat, he replied: "I am Elefterios… the baker," he said. The guard kept his eyes locked for another second, but he said nothing.

Alexi knew he was next and he said nothing while he nervously waited, his stomach turning and his knees starting to shake. He kept his eyes fixed on the ground. It was not until the guard unsheathed his sword slowly that he turned his eyes upward and looked at him. The long drawn sound of scraping metal filled their ears as the blade pulled from the scabbard.

The guard smiled as he turned the blade toward the ground, keeping his grip tight.

"And who is *second* in this group?" he asked – again, quite politely, but with a tinge of sarcasm

"Alexi… a farmer's assistant," the young man replied with a cracked voice after which he immediately returned his gaze downward.

The guard seemed satisfied as he turned to the third man.

"You?" he asked.

"Manoli, sir. I am the *Prokriti*," he said calmly and politely – staring forward and not making eye contact.

"Hmph," the guard groaned. He quickly went to the next man.

"You," he said more as a statement than as a question.

"Yianni, sir. I sell the daily catches at the fish market."

The guard then turned his back to Father Germanos and began to walk away. "I know you, priest. Don't speak," he said coldly.

"Why do you want to speak with the new Disdar?" he asked Elefterios as he approached him at the front of the line.

"*New*?" Elefterios began, "Er... sir, we came to discuss the British man's taking of the Parthenon."

"What of it?" the guard asked indignantly.

"Sir..." Elefterios added, "we came to ask the Disdar to stop him."

At this the guard erupted with a loud, belly shaking laugh that filled the air. The second guard also began to laugh, not because he understood what was causing his partner to laugh, but rather because of how hysterical it was to see him laughing and carrying on.

After a long few seconds, the first guard turned to the second, still laughing, and said in a loud call: "Shall we tell the young Disdar that there are five Greek dogs here to see him? Shall we bring them to him, even though they forgot to make an appointment?" he added with more laughter.

The five Greeks stood expressionless, staring at the ground in silent fear.

The sentry disappeared inside as the first guard kept a distrustful eye on the five men. After a few minutes, which seemed an eternity to the waiting men, the sentry reappeared with a heavy rope in his hands, coiled like the whip hanging from his waist. The men shuddered as they feared what would follow.

"Follow me," he said abruptly, his voice sharp and officious. The five men took a collective deep breath and walked in the guard's footsteps. They entered the guard house and ignored the deathly stare of the main guard as they passed him. They were led down a long corridor, around a corner, down another long corridor, through a much shorter hallway, and into a small rotunda, which opened into a scenic courtyard.

"This way," the sentry said needlessly. "Stay in a straight line and *walk* to the Disdar's office at the *Propylaea*, the gated entrance at the top of the mountain," he said with an even tone.

The five Greeks smiled as they realized that they were going to get to see the Disdar. Elefterios and the others were filled with hope as they took a few quick steps toward the smooth marble stairs that were part of the dusty, pinecone mountain path. Elefterios was excited about taking the trip up the mountain path; he had always dreamed of doing it. Always dreamed of reaching the top and seeing the Parthenon up close. He couldn't help but keep the smile off his face, and the other Greeks shared his joy.

"Wait!" the guard yelled as they all froze in their tracks and turned to look at him. "You'll need this," he said as he dropped the heavy rope to the ground. It was about five inches in diameter and about eighteen feet in length, capped with a heavy metal band on each end to keep it from separating. The Greeks stared at the rope not knowing what the guard meant.

"You must keep both hands on the rope as you climb the path. If so much as one hand lets go – even for a second, even to wipe the sweat off your stinking faces – an archer will kill you."

The men were silent as they eyed the heavy rope and then looked up at the hot sun pounding down on them.

"Do you still want to see the Disdar, you Greek pigs?" he asked teasingly. "Maybe you should all just go home and not come back. It would be unfortunate if you had an accident on that difficult climb up to the Acropolis," he said with an insidious smile.

"No... we're going," Elefterios said, breaking the silence. He bent down and picked up the end of the rope, visibly struggling to lift it to his midsection. A few seconds later, the remaining Greeks joined him and together they carried their burden.

Each of them wished he had a sip of water before they were to begin, but they knew that making such a request might put them in further jeopardy, so they refrained. They wrapped their hands tight around the twine-spun rope, knowing that calloused and bleeding palms and fingers were in their future, and they slowly began the march up the marble path.

Almost instantly their bodies began to betray them. Their heads, backs, and armpits poured out all the water their bodies were desperately trying to maintain. Their stomachs knotted and turned in protest. Their arms feigned their ability to carry the rope. Their hands slowly allowed their skin cover to crack and tear with the twine of the rope. And their knees slowly began conveying a sense of future dereliction.

However unprepared they were for this unexpected burden, they somehow managed to maintain a consistent speed and steady pace as they made their way up the worn steps and through the dusty bramble that they occasionally had to cross. The hot sun and sweat blurred their vision, but Elefterios kept his focus as he led them on.

After nearly an hour of painful climbing, they could finally see the top entrance. They were far too tired to try to speak, but they kept the slow pace Elefterios set. As they reached the last corner, two Turkish archers within a stone's throw of them, took offensive positions and drew their bows back, aiming at the weary Greeks.

"Don't drop the rope...," the first man said. "You've been doing so good, so far." He laughed as he said it.

As Alexi watched the archer in fear, he missed his next step and tripped on a rock lying adjacent to the smooth marble step before him. Everyone stopped instantly, knowing what might happen next.

"Alexi!" yelled Elefterios.

"Hold on! Hold on!" the others yelled simultaneously.

Alexi's right hand kept strong to the rope, but when his feet slid out from under him, so too did his left hand. A thud sounded as his back struck the marble stair and the wind flew from his lungs.

He strained nonetheless with his outstretched left hand, reaching desperately for the rope that had slipped from his non-bleeding hand.

The first archer pulled back his bow and charged forward two steps as he closed his aim in on the young man.

A long second passed until he released the tension and unnotched the arrow – laughing wildly with his companion.

The Greeks stood in shock, glad Alexi was seemingly spared, but they were also pained by the torture and embarrassment they had just endured.

Alexi grabbed the rope tightly with both hands and pulled himself to his feet.

"Are you okay?" Elefterios whispered to him.

"Yes," the whispered response came with bated breath. "Let's go," he urged as they continued their march to the echoes of laughter behind them.

Within minutes the Greeks came to a giant stone gate, where two more guards stood.

"You can drop the rope now," a burly guard instructed them as he approached.

At first, the Greeks did not comply. They were fearful that this was a trick and they paused as they contemplated how to respond.

"Drop the rope!" the guard ordered with authority.

They struggled to tear their blood-soaked hands from the rope, which was now almost a part of their own skin. Their flesh was torn off from the twine as they pulled free in pain and exhaustion.

Their arms ached to the point that they could not raise them even to wipe the sweat from their brows. Father Germanos and Alexi both fell to the ground, their knees finally giving way to the numbness that suddenly enveloped their legs.

The guard exhaled and shook his head in disappointment at them. He then walked over to a post where two horses were hitched and he returned with a wooden bucket of water, splattered with hay and dirt.

"Drink you dogs," he said as he dropped the bucket before them.

Their bloody hands immediately made the water turn red, but they each cupped their hands and drank from the bucket without pause.

The guard pointed to a shaded area and ordered them to wait there until they were called. The men dragged the bucket with them and collapsed when they reached the shade. They each silently prayed that they would be able to recapture their strength, courage and wits.

51

EIGHT

By the time the Greeks were finally called, it was well past the third prayers, the *'Asr,'* as the Muslims called it. The sun had dropped by this point, and the Greeks were able to gather some strength after their long and torturous climb. The Turkish guard was kind enough to bring them a second bucket of water – this time from the horses' trough – which they drank again, but in more measured amounts than before.

Their arms and legs were covered in blood and dirt, their clothes were covered in blood and dirt, and their faces were covered in blood and dirt. They had nothing to wrap their bloodied hands in to protect or clean them, so they all sat with their hands suspended in mid air allowing the wind only to dry them from the stained red water they had used to clean themselves. No one said a word.

The smell of roasted *shawarma* meat suddenly filled their nostrils as they heard a door open from across the guards' station. The Greeks collectively turned and noticed two men emerge, carrying a large tray of bread, rice, olives, and chunks of various cheeses. The stomachs of the weak men immediately began to churn jealously. Alexi was the only one of them who did not turn his eyes to the ground in an attempt at ignoring the scene, he was so hungry and tired that he simply did not have the strength to pull his eyes away from the feast that was just out of his reach.

Alexi watched as the men carefully walked through a small courtyard, and he knew that they were approaching the Disdar's office to take him his afternoon meal. "I am so hungry," he whispered to himself.

Elefterios, Manolis, and Father Germanos quickly whispered back. "*Shush,*" and Alexi dropped his head in defeat; silent again.

After more long minutes, a tall guard with a red sash approached them.

"Get up," he ordered dispassionately.

The Greeks quickly rose and began to pat off their clothes.

"Come with me," the tall guard said as he turned and began to walk off. The Greeks followed dutifully.

They passed a small series of defensive walls until they came to a huge row of steps leading up a small hill. On their left they could see part of a temple wall protruding, on their right another. As they rose up the steps, they could turn and look behind them and see all of Athens below. How beautiful their country was!

Elefterios wished he were given a moment to take it all in, to study, to ponder, to contemplate all that was around him. He never dreamed the view could be so breathtaking, so spectacular. The blue attic sky, with spotted white clouds, majestically hovering over the crystal waters of the Aegean sea. "Just as the ancients must have seen it," he thought to himself.

Upon reaching the top of the stairs, the Greeks were overcome with their first full view of the Parthenon. It towered in the center of the mountain, dominating the entire landscape. A cool breeze enveloped them as they stood staring in awe.

"Athena is welcoming us," Manoli called with a smile.

The men were so overwhelmed, in large part because they had never suspected that the Parthenon was so immense or so perfect in shape and form. Before today, they had only seen the temple from the Athenian streets far below, because the Greeks were strictly forbidden from coming to this military fortress that the Turks guarded so closely.

Never had they imagined the Parthenon was so large and so powerful... so intact. The columns in their perfect order seemed to climb from the ground to hold the angled roof with precision. Even from the distance between them and the temple, they could make out some of the largest sculptures adorning the top of the walls – peering down at them, beckoning them to come and pay them tribute.

The temple sat as if floating on air and the Greeks were awestruck. Elefterios imagined the hand of God Himself, the hand of Zeus as he was known to Elefterios' forefathers, reaching down from heaven to caress the beautiful creation. How proud the Father must be to know that his children were able to build what was clearly a dream.

None of the Greeks commented on the mosque that had been built inside the walls of the Parthenon. None of them seemed capable of even noticing it, as if it were just a temporary playhouse built on the branch of a glorious tree.

"What a blessing by God," Father Germanos stated as he gazed at the temple. "Oh, to be a bird… free to view this beauty whenever I wish," he continued.

The guard turned to them and strongly spoke. "Move it!"

They all tore their eyes from the temple without another glance and noticed a large building amongst some housing to the side. Two, very large warriors stood proudly at each side of the entrance to the main building, both wearing chain-covered breastplates and armor. The first had a metal patch covering his left eye with a helmet that covered what was left of his broken face. They looked like hardened fighters, like seasoned warriors who had fought many a battle. As the Greeks stared, the guards unsheathed their swords waiting for their approach.

"God protect us," Father Germanos silently prayed.

The Greeks stopped in confusion when their escort suddenly turned without a word and walked back toward the stairs. They looked up at the warrior-guards, who were now staring at them with evil intent in their eyes, and they were overcome with the feeling that they were in deadly danger, as if what lay beyond the door these men were guarding were not an office, but rather the fiery pits of hell. Their stomachs and souls seemed to drop instantly, as if they were about to jump off a cliff to their deaths. They couldn't help but shudder in fear at the sight of these ferocious men.

"The Greek dogs are here," one of the two yelled out without moving an eye from the trembling men before them.

A moment later a calm and collected voice replied. "Let them in."

The guard took two enormous steps toward the Greeks and dragged the blade of his sword on the marble floor as he did. The sound shrilled their ears and put more fear in their hearts.

"Remember, *you dogs*, keep your voices quiet or I will take your tongues for roasting tonight!" he threatened ominously. None of the men responded, and none locked eyes with him. They waited quietly until the door was opened by the second guard and they were shuffled in.

It was a large, open room with shelves filled with papers on one side. A large, intricately carved pine desk was on the right. The Disdar, a young man with a young man's beard, sat behind the desk quietly watching them enter.

There were two very large wooden barrels adjacent to his desk with foreign letters painted in black paint on their covers:

HON.LORD-ELGIN
NO.26
- RUM -

The Greeks did not understand the painted words, nor could they guess as to their contents. There also stood a long wooden tube with brass fittings held on a triangular base next to the Disdar's desk. It was pointing out of a window to the west. A small chest sat on the corner of the desk facing the Disdar, and the etched wooden frames of two obscured paintings leaned against the wall behind him. The floor was covered with thick crimson carpets.

When the Disdar rose, the Greeks immediately bowed their heads in respect, saying not a word. The guards stood behind them, breathing hard, as a reminder of their presence in the room – as if the Greeks needed a reminder!

Crossing the carpet to approach them, the Disdar revealed himself as a short, lean man –very young in age- in his early twenties at best. His large *turban*, seemed too big for his little head and frame. Indeed, it seemed nearly to be half his height – as if intentionally inflated to make him seem taller than he actually was. In another situation, he might have seemed comical in his appearance, but to them, at that time and at that place, *he* was their master and there was no room for anything but absolute obedience.

In light of all they had been through and the heavy fear that hung over them now, Elefterios questioned his resolve to even inquire of the Disdar as to what his intentions toward Lord Elgin were. His original enthusiasm seemed to have been beaten out of him in this short time.

The way he had planned for this to happen was not in any way how it was unfolding. The dialogue he'd practiced, the flowery speech lauding the Disdar as the protector of the Greeks' history, now seemed out of place.

Who was he to suggest that the British Lord was trying to trick the Disdar out of the temple? Who was he to suggest that he knew *anything* more than the Disdar? Who was he at all? "Just a Greek dog," he thought to himself as whatever amount of hope remained in his heart disappeared.

"Why have you come to me?" The young Disdar spoke in a calm tone as he approached them.

Elefterios, and all the others, were speechless.

The Disdar smiled, knowing well the trial they had undergone to get before him. "Come, come now," he said. "Tell me. Why have you come to see me?"

The silence hung heavy, but Elefterios knew that he must respond, for no other reason than if he did not, such failure to respond might be construed as an insult – worthy of more punishment.

"Your Excellency," he forced out, his voice straining as he spoke. "Your Excellency, we are but five men before you, but our feelings mirror those of all your Greek subjects." The words seemed to come out of nowhere now, and Elefterios, emboldened, lifted his head slowly and glimpsed at the Disdar as he continued.

"The matter about which we have begged to speak to you surrounds the Englishman, Lord Elgin, and his desire to steal our Parthenon," Elefterios stated with a monotone voice.

"Oh, really?" the Disdar asked inquiringly. Although the Greeks were ignorant of the presents that they had seen in this office, the Disdar knew well that Elgin was a very generous purchaser of his favor. The amazing English telescope that gave him the vision of a hundred men, the jewels on his desk and the other treasures coming his way, and, of course, the casks of that wonderfully fermented drink from a British colony in the Caribbean that he so enjoyed. *"Roooom,"* the British called it.

Elefterios, quickly responded. "Yes, your Excellency, yes. We have heard that Lord Elgin has made false claims that he works under orders from his Great Sublime

Majesty, Sultan, Selim III, himself! We have heard that Elgin claims the right not just to study the Parthenon and to copy the sculptures with mortar, but also the right to tear down the temple, and to take the sculptures onto a ship bound for Britannia. To take them away from their *home!*" he concluded with emphasis.

"Hmmph," the Disdar grunted. "What else have you heard, Greek?"

Elefterios lifted his head again and continued. "There is talk that he wishes to take them to decorate his Scottish castle."

The Disdar frowned and was silent. Elefterios wondered if he had gone too far. He decided to make his last point quickly.

"In any case, your Excellency, the point is that we have come to ask you to stop Lord Elgin from stealing the Parthenon from us. We place our faith in your capable hands."

At this last comment, the Disdar's visage went blank.

"Why is this ancient ruin so important to you Greek?" he asked after a moment.

"The Parthenon is our pride, our history, our legacy, a marker of our past glory. It is a beautiful creation of antiquity. Your Excellency, you would not want to see your most sacred mosque disassembled, would you? Imagine your feelings if you were watching some foreigner take apart such an edifice brick by brick under your nose. Well, that is how we Greeks feel about Lord Elgin taking apart the Parthenon."

The Disdar scowled and cleared his throat.

"Do you mock me, Greek? Whoever would dare to even threaten to destroy a mosque would have his head chopped off his body before the last words even left his lips. And how dare you even *try* to sway me by comparing a mosque to a half-destroyed pagan temple!" His voice gained volume and anger as he continued. "How dare you even question *anything* we do! This is *our* land and you are our slaves, *you Greek dogs!*"

At this, the two guards moved from the back of the room to positions immediately adjacent to the young Disdar.

"Even if I were to give away this precious temple of yours, there would be nothing you could do about it, because it is not yours – it is mine!" He nearly roared in anger as he continued. The guards unsheathed their swords.

At this Father Germanos took a short step forward and bowed in front of the Disdar. The remaining Greeks watched him half in silence and half in fear. The Disdar also watched him and waited. Father Germanos quietly spoke.

"Your Excellency, it was with the greatest respect that we came to you... begging for your ear just to hear us. We are your loyal subjects, and we beg your forgiveness if we have offended you in any way – that was not *in any way* our intention. You are great, the Sultan is greater and *Allah* is even greater still. We hope your anger can pass and that you can accept my words as true. Please forgive us and let us take our leave of you in peace."

The Disdar exhaled and turned his back to the priest. He made a pushing motion with his right hand toward the men and the guards understood that he meant for them to be taken away. They moved toward the Greeks, who, needing no instruction on what to do next, turned and immediately walked toward the door. No one said a word as they exited the office and re-entered the courtyard.

As the door of the Disdar's office slammed shut, the second guard cracked his whip loudly in the air above the men. The Greeks froze and noticed, for the first time, that the guards had laid the heavy rope on the road in front of them again.

"Pick it up and head back down," he called as his whip cracked once again in warning.

Without a word the Greeks retook their prior order, picked up the familiar rope, and began the descent down the mountain. Blood and sweat covered them until they reached the bottom just before dusk. They were relieved they made the last trek without incident, indeed, they were relieved to be alive.

In spite of their torture, each man somehow found the strength to make his way home. But their earlier convictions were shattered and each questioned the logic of pursuing this matter any further. Their spirits and bodies were torn apart on this day, just as were the sculptures from the walls of the temple.

###

When Irini first glimpsed Elefterios limping into their home, she dropped the plate of food she was preparing for Anastasia and rushed to him. Papou Andoni followed seconds later and caught the man as he collapsed from exhaustion. Yia-yia Anastasia lost her breath at the sight of him, and the young girl, too scared and confused to even cry, stood petrified watching the scene unfold.

"The Devils must have dragged him from the back of a horse!" Papou Andoni exclaimed in disgust as he clutched him.

"My God, my God!" Irini cried as tears poured from her eyes and she cradled her husband's head. "My darling, my darling... what happened! My God are you okay?" she cried in a near-shrieking voice full of pain and anger. But Elefterios had no strength to respond with words; he simply looked into her eyes, smiled briefly, and then passed out.

"He's alive, he's alive!" Yia-yia Anastasia cried in joy as she saw him smile at her daughter. "He's alive and *home*, praise God almighty! He is alive and home! Everything is going to be fine now. Everything is going to be fine." She then turned to her granddaughter, who still stood in shock, and grasped her hands in delight. "He's alive, child, your father is *alive*. Rejoice, rejoice!" The grandmother was almost dancing in delight as she held the child's hands tightly.

But the young girl could not even manage a smile. As her grandmother danced, hugged and cooed over her in joy, the girl could only stare at her mother, who was wailing in fear and pain a few feet away.

Overwhelmed by the combination of emotions around her, and within her, the girl took one more look at her dirty, beaten and bloodied father and passed out, joining him in the safe haven of the subconscious, where they could both escape and heal their wounds.

NINE

"The Disdar cares nothing for Greek history, Greek antiquities, or us Greeks," Elefterios whispered in disgust. "He's too young, too vain, and too full of anger and contempt for us to care," he continued as his breath gave out. "Why am I limiting this description to just *him*?" he asked himself aloud. "No, the *Turks* care nothing about us. We are their slaves, their talking dogs," he stated coldly.

Irini "shooshed" him to be quiet and spoon fed him more *avgolémono* soup. The chicken and lemon combination soothed his throat, and the warm broth comforted his still-aching limbs.

"I will *not* shoosh!" he said with some authority as he pushed himself to sit upright in his bed. "I wish his father, the old Disdar, had not died. Perhaps *he* would have listened to me. Perhaps things would have gone differently," he said with a heavy tone in his voice.

"Nothing would have been different, Lefteri," Irini quickly responded as she urged him to settle. "And nothing will ever be different while we remain slaves," she quietly added as the truth of her words silenced them both.

It was three days since he had returned from the Parthenon. He had slept for the entire first day, Irini bathing and caring for his wounds all the while. The honey-herb ointment that covered his hands caused him a little discomfort now, but he did not complain. How could he when it seemed that every waking moment of his day was filled with "praise God that he is alive" cheers from his mother-in-law? Elefterios knew she was right and that he was, indeed, lucky to be alive. He also knew, as did his wife, that the future of his people and the protection of their history could not come from anyone other than themselves. They were to be their own saviors; their only saviors.

Three days passed in this fashion as Elefterios healed, and he and Irini contemplated their existence as Greeks dogs in the *Ateni Samjak*. During this period of healing and contemplation, none of the other men in their group had made contact with him except for his brothers, whom Irini personally visited at Elefterios' insistence. All the men were healing, physically, but none emotionally. They were beaten on the inside and out. They were defeated. All except for Elefterios.

On the fourth day after his return, Elefterios declared himself fit and returned to the bakery. His hands had healed enough to let him mix the ingredients and with the help of Papou Andoni, who would knead the dough and roll it into loaves for him, he was able to have a full day's production. At no point did he slow in his work and at no point did he complain of any pain or discomfort.

Neither Irini, nor any of his family commented on his decision to return so quickly to work – they simply accepted it. They wanted him to take more time to fully heal, but they were torn because they felt, somehow, that they now lacked the authority to question his decisions.

They could not explain it exactly, but the ordeal with the Disdar had transformed Elefterios. Like Odysseus on his trip to Hades *and back,* and like Jonah from the belly of the whale, Elefterios had been reborn to a new strength. He was more than what he had been before. He carried himself with a silent confidence that exuded strength, control and intelligence. The impetuousness of his youth had vanished, and the boy who once was - was now a complete man, an *"olorkrilos andras,"* as his mother-in-law proudly referred to him now.

The change in him was perceived by more than just his immediate family - the other Greeks noticed his transformation as well. There was a sense of awe about him, an admiration for him that had not existed before. He had looked into the eyes of the devil, but he stood tall and refused to cower in fear. It was *respect* that the Athenian Greeks gave him now. Respect for the man he had proven himself to be.

That night, at dinner, he announced to his family that he was going to see the Voivode the next day.

Yia-yia Anastasia gasped and dropped her fork at his statement. "What? What did you say?" she exclaimed. "You're not even healed from your last encounter with the Turks!" "You can't, Elefterios, you can't!" she pleaded. "By the grace of God you

61

are back with us. Please don't leave again!"

Irini and Papou Andoni said nothing -they simply looked at Elefterios and waited for him to respond.

"Baba?" little Anastasia asked in a meek voice.

"Yes, my sweet," he said, as everyone turned to look at her.

"Are they going to kill you tomorrow, Baba?" she asked as her lower lip began to tremble and tears began to form in her eyes.

He rose from his seat and quickly knelt next to his daughter's chair, cupping her face in his hands and lovingly staring into her eyes as he spoke. "Only God knows our fate, little one. Only God can decide when it is our time to leave this earth. And until that day, we must do what we believe is right. What we believe *He* wants us to do. We must have faith that He is guiding us toward our destiny. And we must not take the easy path, we must take only the path that is right, however hard it may be and however harsh the consequences may be in following that path. I am not afraid of what God has planned for me, child, and you cannot be afraid either." His voice was so sincere and loving that the child was calmed before he even finished his last words and kissed her forehead.

Irini was also calmed by his words. She, too, felt that fate was calling him, and her, forward. "*Amen*," she added as he retook his seat.

"The will of God will be," Yia-yia Anastasia said without another glance at the others.

Papou Andoni was silent for long while before he asked, "Son, do you need to see the Voivode *tomorrow* ? Can't you wait a few days to get your strength completely back? Can't you wait until the others are fit to join you?"

"No," said Elefterios simply. "I am strong enough, and I am going alone."

At that comment, the elder Anastasia quietly placed her utensils on her plate and hurried to the bedroom without a word. The echoes of her reverent prayers filled their ears as they finished their dinner without another word.

TEN

But for the bumps of the tires striking the occasional pot holes in the road, the taxi ride from the hotel was a quiet event. The grandfather knew that the story was too much for the boy to fully comprehend, but it had to be told to him now. Now and again, and again until it was part of him.

As the boy grew into manhood, he would be able to understand all the parts of the story that were beyond his present years. As he grew, he would memorize the story, verbatim, and pass it on - just as the grandfather had done to the boy's father and now, through a sad twist of fate, to his grandson.

The tradition of passing down stories orally from one generation to the next was all but lost in this modern world. People today are so dependent upon the written word – usually the *electronically* written word – that they are unable to even fathom how the oral tradition worked for so many thousands of years. Modern man's limitations though, were self imposed. The human mind had abilities far beyond what most people could ever imagine.

It was thus in keeping with this tradition that he now passed on this story to the boy. He did not know exactly why, but in all his life he had never felt it was right for *him* to memorialize the story. He had never felt it was *his* role to share it with the world. Had he ever felt otherwise at any point over all these decades, he could easily have written it down himself, but he believed that his role was to carry the torch and pass it on to the next runner, not to cross the finish line himself.

His son, Paul, believed his role was to memorialize the story. He had long discussions with his father over the need to write the story down. He spoke with reverence at Homer and how he had taken the oral history of Odysseus to a world audience, an audience that continues to grow day by day. He felt so strongly about passing on the story to the world that in spite of his father's protestations, he was convinced that it was the course he was destined to follow. Shortly after beginning this task, however, he died in a car crash. Ironically, the crash came when he was passionately dictating the story to his smart phone and driving a dangerous road.

It was a sad irony to the old man that his son's death resembled, at least in part, that of another author, Paul the Apostle; perhaps the most well-known author who has ever lived. The disciple who died for, amongst other "crimes," writing down a story.

The explosion that followed the crash destroyed both man and machine and nearly this story with it. That was the danger in keeping the oral tradition. The stories were as fragile as were the men and women who kept them.

To the old man, it was a blessing and a curse to be passing on this story again. The process would take years, as it did for Michael to learn it. For the boy to learn the story, it would have to be told and retold hundreds of times, and the boy would have to tell it to him hundreds of times as well – to ensure that he knew every last syllable, in perfect order.

The old man constantly prayed to God for the strength he needed to accomplish this one last task.

He turned his gaze to the boy sitting next to him. Konstantine was staring out of the window in a daydream, reliving, no doubt, the story he had heard up to this point.

"I don't understand what he's doing, Papou," Konstantine said angrily as he shook his head. "The va-vo-di is going to kill him for sure," he said matter of factly.

"Well, you'll know soon enough, boy," the old man said comfortingly, as he patted him on his leg. "All in time... all in time," he concluded.

"Why are we going to the museum again, Papou? This is our third trip since you began to tell me the story," the boy asked with a slightly annoyed tone in his voice.

"It's our last trip here, boy," he replied. "We are leaving for Athens tomorrow morning."

The taxi pulled up to the drop-off zone in front of the British Museum. The old man paid the driver and then exited with his grandson. He paused as they approached the first guard station and exhaled as he looked at the grand museum in front of him.

"Let's go see our history," Konstantine said as he grasped his grandfather's hand.

The old man looked down at him and smiled. He squeezed the boy's hand tightly and together they made their approach.

ELEVEN

The next afternoon, Father Germanos slowly made his way to the bakery, one hand clutching a cane, the other holding firm to his Bible. He was sweating, out of breath and tired, very tired. His bandaged hands were still sore and made his trip difficult. The shooting pain he experienced as he walked forced him to constantly switch his cane and Bible between hands. The hot sun added to his burden, and the combination of these conditions caused the memory of his torture from the Turks to occupy most of his thoughts. By the time he arrived at the bakery he had a throbbing headache and was near collapse.

"You know," he said without preamble as he laid his Bible on the counter and clutched it for support, "if it's true that the Sultan is fully aware of Lord Elgin's activities, you are likely to get no further with the Governor of Athens than we did with the General of the Acropolis. Even if the Voivode has authority over the Disdar - and I am not sure that he does - the Sultan rules them both and us all, and if the Sultan has given the Englishman the right to take the Parthenon, then the Voivode will be powerless to stop him. That is, presuming that he would actually *want* to stop him – and why would he?" he asked incredulously. "The Voivode will certainly have no more interest in the preservation of Greek history than that young Devil did." There was a pause as he continued.

"Elefterios," he implored as he inched closer to him, "I am afraid that your persistence will not be rewarded. Elefterios..." and a long pause followed, "I am afraid of the risks associated with what you now intend to do."

"I know," Elefterios agreed quietly in response. "I know, *Pater*, I know... more than you think," he concluded cryptically.

The statement was not missed by the priest. "What are you *not* telling me Elefterios?" he inquired in earnest. The two men had been friends long enough and certainly had been through enough struggles together to share a deep level of trust. Over the years they had held many dialogues over the holy text, philosophy, ancient Greece, and, in relative silence, over their fate and existence under Turkish occupation. The last ordeal they had suffered, rather than dividing them, in fact, made their relationship stronger. They were brothers.

Father Germanos repeated his question. "What are you not telling me, Elefterios?"

After a little pause, Elefterios responded. "It's probably nothing, but I can't seem to shake something that happened last night." Without needed further prompting he continued.

"Irini and I were deep in slumber when I could just *feel* that something was watching me. I wasn't being watched by some demon or by someone with an intent to harm me, but, I don't know, somehow, even though I was sleeping, I could just feel that I was being watched," he said. "It stirred me enough to wonder if I was dreaming or if I was awake. So I forced myself to break free from the sleep, shook my head and opened my eyes to see little Anastasia standing next to Irini, who was sleeping soundly. "Mama? Mama?" she called in a panic, "Is Baba all right? Is he alive?"

Before I could react, Irini was immediately awake and responding, as mothers are somehow always able to do with their children. "Of course he is child," Irini said quickly as she reached for the girl. A split second later though, Irini turned to look for me in the bed. I saw the corner of her eye that very first second she looked for me, and *Father,* I don't know that she was certain that I was there. In that same instant I saw Anastasia's eyes peering over me, through me, as if I were not there. As if only her mother were lying in that bed. For that second, I felt empty. For that second, I wasn't sure if I was even alive."

He paused for a moment, then looked up at his friend. "Where are my manners? Let me get you some water and a coffee, and then we can continue this discussion," he said as he quickly turned and went to the back of the bakery to prepare what he had offered. Father Germanos pulled up a chair next to the counter and slowly sat down, relieved by his friend's courtesy, but troubled by his vision.

When Elefterios returned, he placed the tray with the two coffees and waters before the priest and continued from where he had left off.

"So after that moment when I felt like a spirit of the dead watching my wife and daughter search for me, I wondered what it meant. Before I could really think anything more about it though, Irini found my hand, squeezed it tight, and told the child to look at me and to see me lying next to her."

"'Baba? Baba!,' the child cried as she jumped over her mother and crawled next to me, hugging me deeply in relief as she spoke. 'Baba, I had a bad dream; a horrible dream. I dreamed that something awful happened to you. That some bad Turks hurt you and that you died.' The child was sobbing through her words, and she soon broke down entirely, racked by tears."

"'I am fine, my sweet, I am fine,' I told her lovingly as I hugged and hugged her. 'Everything is fine. Your mind is playing tricks on you. There is nothing to worry about. I am right here and I am fine.' Irini *shushed* and *shooed* her as she patted her head and stroked her long hair comfortingly. A minute later, the child was fast asleep. And the next day, she remembered none of it."

"God speaks to us in mysterious ways," the priest responded in a quiet but confident tone. "The question now is whether you will listen."

"But which instructions do I follow, *Pater?*" Elefterios pleaded. "To those from the dream voice of my child, or to those I feel in my heart and my very soul. That which burns me and calls me to fight. To fight not just to stop this Englishman from robbing our antiquities, but that which urges me to fight for our freedom!" his voice rose a decibel at this last comment.

"Quiet, Lefteri, quiet!" the priest whispered.

Elefterios continued without delay, but he did so cognizant of his friend's warning and so the loudness of his speech returned to a conversational tone.

"And what of her dream?" he rhetorically asked. "Was her dream really nothing to worry about? Was it just the product of a scared child afraid of and still dealing with the horrible sight of her father having been so cruelly beaten just a few days earlier? Was it just a natural reaction to how her little mind was dealing with that event? Or was it an omen, a warning of what is to come?"

"God speaks to us in mysterious ways, Lefteri" the priest repeated. "Through dreams, visions, burning bushes, oracles and, sometimes, through the mouths of babes. You must pray to Him and ask for guidance on choosing the right path in front of you."

"I have, *Pater,*" Elefterios responded quickly, "and he has told me not to be afraid of my future. Not to be a coward. He has told me to stand up as a man and face my demon, *our* demons."

"And if it means your death?" the priest asked.

"Then my fate will be no worse than that of our Lord and Savior, Jesus Christ."

With that and with no other words, Elefterios stood to exit the bakery. Just as he grabbed the handle of the front door, the sound of marching feet and clapping horse hooves filled their ears. In an instant, five of the Sultan's Janissary Guards with swords drawn surrounded the exit to the street, having so swiftly dismounted from their horses and simultaneously armed themselves, that Father Germanos hardly could follow their movements with his eyes.

Elefterios stood tall with his chin held high and arms to his side, but otherwise motionless as he faced them.

"Are you the baker?" the lead Janissary Guard asked Elefterios in an apathetic monotone.

Elefterios looked him in the eyes and responded: "Yes, I am."

"The one from the City?" the guard asked again.

"I am Elefterios *Politis* – a Greek man from Constantinople... *the City.*"

With a twitch of his left hand fingers and a curious whistle, the guard summoned a donkey that was previously obscured by the large horses of the Janissaries. The little donkey, no taller than any of the men, obeyed its master and trotted dutifully next to the guard before completely coming to a stop.

"Get on," the guard ordered Elefterios.

Without a word of protest, Elefterios mounted the donkey and clasped the leather reins draped over its shoulders. The Janissaries instantly sheathed their swords and mounted their horses. The lead guard led the phalanx formation, with two mounted guards in front of and two behind Elefterios on the donkey. Without a word they trotted off – leaving the priest alone in the bakery.

As he watched the procession leave, Father Germanos noticed the fearful and silent stares of many villagers peering through the cracks in their windows and doors at the scene as it concluded. He also noticed the last Janissary guard turn and look back at the bakery curiously and for a long moment. An odd stare, the priest thought to himself, as the guard then shook his head and turned back to his prisoner.

As he watched Elefterios disappear into the distance, he made the sign of the cross three times quickly in his direction. "May God bless and keep you my son… *my friend*," the priest said.

TWELVE

When they arrived at the Governor's mini-palace at the port, the sun was just beginning to set. Horse-mounted guards traveled in pairs along the dusty road leading to the docks, which were busy with mariners loading and unloading their cargo. Orange sunbeams danced in the crystal blue waters to form thousands of sparkling stars at the crest of every wave. The warmth of the sun's rays comforted Elefterios. He breathed in the salty air in a calm and steady rhythm.

"I am yours Lord. Do with me as you wish," he quietly spoke before his thoughts were interrupted by the lead guard abruptly stopping the procession and dismounting. As the other Jannisaries dismounted, a dozen young men instantly appeared to attend to the horses and Elefterios' donkey.

In an instant, Elefterios found himself surrounded by the Jannisaries and being led through the main gate of the palace entrance into an unknown garden in full bloom. He was too rushed to pay careful attention to the actual species, but the sweet smells and bright colors of the flowers captured his senses as nature gave him his second reminder that there is beauty in this world, not just barbarism.

They stopped when they came to the enormous wooden doors that were protected by two fierce looking military guards. The Janissary leader waived his hand at the guards, as if motioning them to open the doors and step aside. Without any hesitation, the guards turned to unlock the doors and stepped aside to allow them entrance.

In that brief moment, Elefterios noticed for the first time a white orchid hanging from a lush green tree branch close to his side. It seemed to be smiling at him and beckoning him to caress its petals and inhale its sweet fragrance. As he moved toward it, the last Janissary guard whispered to him *in Greek:* "Don't." It was a quiet, non-threatening warning; almost friendly. It was the opposite of an order, both in tone and in sentiment. It was *protective*.

That half-second warning caused Elefterios to withdraw immediately from his pursuit of the orchid and to turn his eyes to those of that Janissary guard. The guard did not return the look, but he felt the connection being made by Elefterios and he knew that he was finally reunited with his long-lost brother.

"The blessings of the Lord come at mysterious times," Elefterios thought to himself as the doors swung open and he was rushed in with the others.

Before Elefterios could take in his surroundings, he was violently struck in the back of his knees by the scabbard of one of the Governor's military guards – instantly causing him to fall to the ground in a kneeling position. The Janissary guards neither said nor did anything at this, but instead simply moved to one side of the room to observe.

Elefterios recoiled at the searing pain that shot from his toes to his hips, but a sharp intake of breath was the only sound that escaped his lips. His knees began to burn as the pain from striking the stone floor shot though his body an instant later. He closed his eyes for a moment and clenched his teeth as he fought to subdue the pain and remain silent.

When the pain subsided and Elefterios was able to look around, his eyes were filled with the lavish furnishings in the hall of the very wealthy Governor. The stone floor was covered with huge carpets, intricately woven in repeating floral designs, featuring roses, lilacs, hyacinths, tulips and carnations. Each carpet was closed on its ends with gold-colored tassels. Man-size, hand-painted clay pots with large, single-trunk palm trees stood at each side of a large, throne-like chair. The chair was expertly carved in all spots other than those covered by the plush seat and back, which looked by be woven of silk. This was indeed a palace, he thought to himself.

The last rays of the day's sun streamed in from a series of open windows. Rows of candles and torches in wall sconces were lit along all the back walls. As Elefterios watched the flames flicker and shift with the slight breeze coming through, he noticed the large tapestries that hung on the walls depicting famous historical and religious events.

One tapestry, an enormous piece that covered the lengthy wall behind the Governor's throne, depicted the Turkish conquest of Trebizond, the last Christian stronghold to fall to the Turks after Constantinople fell in 1453. With incredible detail, the tapestry displayed the City of Constantinople with its famous Hagia Sophia Greek Orthodox Church and the obelisk of Theodosius prominently displayed, but all under Turkish military control.

On the opposite side of the tapestry across from Hagia Sophia, the port city of Trebizond sat on the Black Sea. It was woven in a blood-black thread that made one feel as if the sea were actually in motion. Turkish tents surrounded the city, as Turkish warriors engaged in battle with the Greeks, who defended in vain. From his distance, he strained to differentiate the Greek warriors from the Turkish ones. At this point the realization of his own brother's duality struck him and he turned to see if Michali was still in the room.

When Elefterios found his brother, they locked stares for a long moment, each quietly considering the other. Memories of shared childhood experiences and questions as to how each had lived since their forced separation crossed each of their minds.

Years flashed between them in those few seconds.

The Voivode's entrance into the room instantly broke the men's stares and captured everyone's immediate attention. He entered through a rear door obscured by two tapestries, accompanied by a Pasha sent by the Sultan himself to oversee the Janissary Corps. The Voivode was a short, heavy man with a long, full beard. His hair was carefully tucked into a large, black turban that matched his cape and shoes. The Pasha was a virtual opposite spectacle: tall, thin, clean-shaven, and wearing gold-colored robes and a matching turban.

The Voivode swiftly strode toward Elefterios, as if he were a wolf falling upon a lame rabbit. Elefterios lifted his head and watched him approach, anticipating that he would be pummeled by the man or worse. Instead, about a foot before reaching him, the Voivode abruptly stopped and looked at his wounded prey. A crooked smile crossed his face as his eyes glared at Elefterios'.

"Why are you here, *Baker* ?" he asked the kneeling man.

"I am here at your call, Sir," Elefterios responded in a clear and steady voice – devoid of any fear.

"No," the Voivode said in a pleasant voice that transformed into an angry tone as he continued, "you are here because you have offended our English friends. You are here because they have protested your actions to the Sultan himself. You are here because they have called for your death and have asked that I carry out the sentence!"

Elefterios did not react whatsoever to this. He remained on his knees, staring at the man before him in complete silence.

"Did you hear me *Baker*?" the Voivode asked.

"I did, sir."

"Now the Pasha is here accompanied by his Janissaries, and they want to know why I have let you go on as you have for so long. They want to know why I let a Greek insult the friend of Selim the Third, Sultan of Sultans, his Majesty, our Emperor, our Lord. Tell me, *Baker*, why have you done this?"

Elefterios responded again in a clear and confident voice. "I have not offended the Sultan, the Disdar, the Pasha, you, or any other Islamic man. I have only asked for consideration to not allow the Parthenon to be cut to pieces and taken away to England. I asked respectfully and humbly... I meant no offense."

"*You meant no offense?*" he responded sarcastically as his voice rose in volume. "Who are you to ask for anything?"

Elefterios bowed his head slightly before responding. "I am just a man," he said.

The Voivode paused before continuing. "Defend yourself, Greek. Tell me why I should not show favor to our English allies and put you to death."

Michali watched fearfully as Elefterios was preparing to reply. He knew that his brother's life would be decided by his answer.

"You can do with me what you will, sir. I meant no offense."

The Voivode turned from Elefterios hastily and sat upon his throne-chair in the center of the room. He smiled deeply as he looked at him, still kneeling before him.

"So what would you have me do, Baker? Teach you manners because you don't understand how your actions offend men? Are you even capable of being taught... are any of you Greeks? You are just supposed to make bread. Nothing else. Make bread and live quietly in your corner of *Ateni Samjak*. *Nothing else*. And yet, *you* have made it your business to interfere with the property and interests of the Sultan." He shook his head in feigned helplessness, raising his eyebrows and arms upward in the universal shrug of expressing '*Why?*'

"Let me tell you what you have done. You have stood up to your masters and demanded that they recognize *your* rights to preserve *your* temple, *your* history. You have ignited a fire in your fellow Greeks that we have suppressed for many generations. Prometheus was your god who did this first, correct? The bringer of fire to the men of caves, the bearer of knowledge to the unschooled. Do you consider yourself Prometheus? Are you a god to your Greeks?" he asked rhetorically. "The Baker god?" he concluded with a smirk that caused all the Turks in the room to laugh loudly - all but one Jannisary who stood absolutely silent and on guard.

When the laughter died down, the Voivode turned again to Elefterios and repeated his question. "So are you Prometheus?" he asked dryly.

"I am nothing but a man. A man who is blessed to be alive. A man who can recognize the wonders of the world around him. The miracles of life now and the extraordinary achievement of our ancient past."

"Are you a priest, a prophet, or a baker?" the Voivode asked sarcastically as light laughter filled the room.

"I am a humble man who means you no disrespect," Elefterios stated and added nothing further. The Voivode contemplated for a moment before continuing.

"Why does this Parthenon matter to you?" he asked with sincerity; his voice lowering to an near whisper, almost as if he were attempting to have a private conversation with Elefterios. "Why do you risk your very life for it?"

Elefterios was torn. He knew that if he told the Voivode the real significance of the Parthenon to him, the true symbolism the temple manifested for him and for all the Greeks, that he would be killed. He knew that if he told him how the Parthenon stood as a reminder of the greatness of his people and as an inspiration for them to recapture that ancient glory, that he would be killed. He knew that telling too much truth would not only spell his doom, but would also guarantee that the Parthenon would be torn apart and destroyed. And so he omitted the complete answer and told only a portion of the truth.

"I honestly never thought that my simple request to the Disdar would have been interpreted as it has been. I never thought..." he said with a long pause, "that I would find myself where I am now, simply by asking for some consideration," Elefterios concluded solemnly as he turned his gaze toward the carpet on the floor directly in front of him.

The Voivode paused again to contemplate the response. "And what of the Disdar?" he asked almost rhetorically. "Why did you feel you had the right to ask him for anything? Was it pride, arrogance or just stupidity that caused you to feel that you were his equal and could ask *anything* of him?"

"It must have been stupidity," Elefterios responded.

"Well, the Disdar thinks it was *pride*, not stupidity! He has informed me that he thinks you want more than your God has allotted for you in this life and, even more, that you feel *entitled* to it. The English have suggested that you view yourself not as an equal of us Turks, but actually *superior* to us. They say you marvel so at this old temple because you wonder how much better your life would be if your ancestors were still in power today. They say that you are spreading seeds of insurrection with the other Greeks, telling them how wonderful your lives would be without your Turkish lords. How great your society and democratic government would be, and how intelligent and enlightened all of you Greeks would be.

"The Englishman warned the Disdar that your fight to stop him from taking the temple, was not about the English threat or even the temple itself, but really was only an excuse for you to create hope in your people and an expectation that they might be more than the slaves they are today; more than livestock or trained animals. The Englishman told this also to the Sultan, and... here we are. So tell me, is he right, baker-philosopher-god-king? Is this all really about you Greeks getting your freedom?"

After a brief pause, Elefterios responded in the same clear and controlled voice as before. "No. I have not ever said such things to any man, and I have certainly made no attempt to create a revolution against you or the Sultan."

The Voivode laughed heartily. "Allah surprises me every day! Perhaps tomorrow he will send me a talking camel, but today he sent me a Greek philosopher!" At his conclusion, the room again broke out into laughter. The Voivode turned again to Elefterios before issuing his sentence.

"You are indeed a wise man, in spite of your being Greek, and I now understand why the Englishman fears you. *I* do not and the *Sultan* certainly does not, but nonetheless, I am going to punish you for your spiritual defiance of your Master's authority. By punishing you, I am also sending a strong message to all the other Greeks who might be thinking similar thoughts as you."

The Voivode then turned to his guards and spoke. "Drag him through the streets of his village so all can see the fate of this rebel, then take him back to the Disdar with instructions to grant the Englishman his request."

With that, the Voivode dismissed them from his palace and before he knew it, Elefterios found himself being carried out of the room and back to the dusty road leading to the port.

Michali cringed as a rope was tied to Elefterios' wrists and secured to the saddle of the lead Janissary guard's horse. He prayed that his brother had enough strength to run steadily all the way back to town. He knew from past experience that the lead guard was never going to break stride. He knew that one slip would result in his brother being dragged to his death - a horrible end that few could ever avoid.

THIRTEEN

Elefterios had managed to keep up with the steady trot of the Janissary Corps. for nearly an hour before he finally tripped and fell.

They were only a few minutes out from the center of town when Elefterios began to notice the Greek townsfolk emerging from their homes and businesses to watch him being marshaled into town like a savage and dangerous criminal being brought to justice.

His breathing was heavy. His brow was full of sweat. His wrists ached from the tight rope. His legs were beginning to betray him. It took all of Elefterios' attention to stay as one with the guards. The rhythm of his strides and breath echoed those of the hooves striking the ground. He was one with the men and horses as they traveled steadily on. He was part of them.

The speed of the procession kept Elefterios unable to focus on any one person along the road, until he saw a small child staring out at him from an open window. It was a little girl named Maria, whom he recognized from the bakery, where she had come many times with her grandmother, also named Maria. Their eyes locked, and he saw the absolute fear that filled the child's visage. It seemed that time stopped for that one moment that she stared at him. In that instant he could sense all the questions and concerns that she had for him. He could almost read them.

As he stared, her face transformed into that of his own daughter, and he was about to call to her when Maria's grandmother suddenly appeared from the side and blocked her view of the events. It was then, as Elefterios looked back at the now-closing window, that he stepped awkwardly upon two rocks, lost his footing, and crashed to the ground. He almost instantly rolled horizontally, smashing his knees, stomach, and face to the ground in virtual unison. This caused the pull-horse to jerk to an immediate stop as its momentum was halted.

The lead Jannisary guard felt the strong pull of his horse as it reared up in protest at the dead weight it was now pulling. He looked back and saw Elefterios spin and tumble as a spurt of blood shot from his mouth upon impact with the ground.

Michali watched with lost breath, but neither said nor did anything in response. His eyes betrayed his concern, though, and the lead Jannisary guard did not miss the pain his fellow guard was experiencing. No one had to tell him what their relationship was, though. He knew. He had experienced it himself when the Corps. had been sent to his own village in the northern mountains en route to *Istanbul – the "City" – Constantinople,* just a few years earlier. He knew the pain that all of them felt at being kidnapped and stolen from their families as children and being forcefully converted to Islam, forced to join an elite Turkish military organization, and brainwashed into believing that protecting the life and interests of the Sultan was their only obligation on this earth.

Though none of the Jannisaries could ever openly confess their true feelings or share any memories of their Greek childhood and families, as that was punishable by death, each of them burned inside at their loss and each longed for a world where they were not slaves.

It was based on these shared emotions that each Jannisary found himself moved by Elefterios' words and action before the Governor. His fearlessness in the face of death was inspiring to them.

At this thought, the lead guard did something that none of the other Jannisaries had ever seen before. Instead of kicking his steed into action and urging it to drag the prisoner forward, as was the common practice, he kept the horse at a dead stop. Michali watched in wonder and exchanged questioning glances with his leader to confirm that the stop was intentional. The other Jannisaries did the same. The leader, however, did not look at any of them, instead, he turned his eyes back to the road and simply sat and waited. All the Janissaries followed suit in what to some observers seemed a clear indication of their respect for Elefterios. They were not going to drag him. Not him.

They waited several minutes in that continued vigil, until it was clear to the leader that Elefterios was back on his feet and standing strong. At that time, instead of resuming the rapid pace they had maintained earlier, the pace he set was that of a fast walk only. At no point further did he race Elefterios into the center of town. He knew what fate awaited him and he did not feel any need *or obligation* to add to that suffering.

"Let him enter town as a man," he thought to himself. "He has earned that right."

As they neared the bakery, the street before them was filled with villagers quietly watching them pass. They gave way for the Jannisaries to continue their trot toward the center of town, where the Disdar and a regiment of his guards stood waiting to receive them.

The young Disdar was excited and overcome with goosebumps as he noticed their approach. The Baker was covered in dirt and blood, his hair a matted mess and his clothes torn severely. The Disdar smiled at the sight.

When they neared the Governor's party, the Jannisaries came to a quick stop, dismounted instantly, and collected the reins of their horses. The lead Jannisary untied the rope binding Elefterios to his horse and stood holding it as Michali took their horses to the side. The Disdar motioned for his two main guards to take the rope, which they did with a jump. At this, the Jannisaries stepped to the side of the street and stood guard, each with one hand on his sword. They were silent sentinels again.

It was then that Elefterios noticed Irini emerge at the front of the crowd, with Father Germanos and Manoli at her side. She was shaking from fear and her eyes were blood red, full of hatred and tears. At the sight of her, he smiled and was filled with joy.

Then the strong pull of the rope-chain on his hands jerked him forward and his eyes fell back upon the same two guards he had met the previous week at the Acropolis. The larger of the two pulled slowly on the rope-chain, hand over hand, smiling as he drew Elefterios near. The second simply unhinged the leather-thronged-whip from his belt and inched forward, slightly licking his lips in anticipation.

There was an energy in the town center of *Ateni Samjak* that day; something that had not been felt there in hundreds of years. An almost palpable sense of fear and anger, of concern and anticipation that was felt by both the Greeks and the Turks. The Disdar's guards were put off at having to push back at the crowds that were pressing in, something that they were completely unaccustomed to doing, and the level of angry voices began to steadily increase from the back of the crowd forward. The guards found themselves turning and facing the Greeks, drawing their swords and threatening their lives if they did not silence and stay themselves.

Irini, Father Germanos and Manoli stood arm in arm at the center of the group, crying, cringing and praying.

The Janissaries remained statuesque in silent observation.

The young Disdar with his oversized turban stood in the shade of a gigantic olive tree surrounded by several guards. He felt so empowered by this event; so honored. What a wonderful opportunity this was for him to establish his complete control over these subjugated people. What a wonderful opportunity this was for him to demonstrate his value to the Voivode, the Sultan, *and* to his English benefactor. He was certainly going to take full advantage of the situation. He smiled warmly, clearly pleased with his good fortune.

As best he could, Elefterios tried to keep himself upright as he was pulled forward. He remembered in a flash the brutal treatment he had endured at the hands of this same guard. He caught sight of the second guard with the leather whip and wondered if that whip was to be his fate after all. As he neared them, the Disdar quickly stepped forward between his guards and raised his hands to silence the crowd.

The Disdar spoke in a high-pitched voice, which he projected more to the crowd than he did to Elefterios. His arm movement and hand gestures were flamboyant and by design meant to emphasize certain parts of his speech as he had practiced and was anxious to deliver to the crowd now.

"Baker! What have you done to your fellow Greeks? What have you done?" the Disdar began dramatically. His last rhetorical question was accompanied by a palms-up gesture, a nod of his head, and a look to the stars for an answer. "Why have you insulted the Sultan?" he demanded.

Elefterios tried to clear his throat to respond but was pulled forcefully by the rope-chain and silenced before he could utter a word.

"You believe you are greater than your fellow Greeks. You believe you are greater than our English friends. You believe you are greater than the Turks of *Ateni Samjak* and the rest of the Turks in the Ottoman Empire. You believe you are greater than the Voivode, the Pasha, the Jannisaries, and even his Most Excellency, the Lord of us all, Selim III, the Sultan and Ruler on High!" His voice strained at the mention of the Sultan, and a clear sense of incredulity accompanied his words at this, demonstrating his shock at Elefterios' gall and disrespect to their Supreme Leader.

"You are better than all of us, *eh* Baker? You are a would-be philosopher and king, *eh*? A protector of your people? A reborn ancient Greek god?" At this the Disdar laughed out loud. "*You* have decided that *you* have the right to judge your masters. To bite the hand that not only feeds you, but allows you to live! *You* have decided that the lives of all these villagers should be sacrificed to teach the rest of the Greeks in the Turkish Empire to respect their Turkish masters!" At this, gasps of awe were heard from the crowd. The Greeks did not know whether they were all to be massacred or whether it was just going to be Elefterios. The guards readied their swords. The Jannisaries also unsheathed their swords and took fighting stances.

The Greek families in the crowd began to hug each other for strength and for protection. The fathers gathered their wives and children behind them, as if ready to stand as a shield to the onslaught that was coming. The elderly tried to shuffle back through the crowd to find safety in their homes. They all knew that their lives were in peril.

The Disdar's threat was real and the Greeks of *Ateni Samjak* knew that a massacre was possible. The threat of death was what kept them in line. That fear was what kept all the Greeks submissive and silent. The Turks had butchered hundreds of thousands of Greeks over the centuries and in the process razed thousands of churches, homes and even entire villages. Laid them all to dust. They raped, pillaged, and enslaved their captives and re-named the lands they forcibly took. These were not myths. These were truths.

The goal of the ever expanding Turkish-Ottoman Empire was always the same, to take physical and *emotional* control of their victims. To erase all memory of their past lives, and to sever their connection with any past glories or achievements of their elders. To eviscerate even their ability to dream of past glories or to hope for a better future. To snuff out their spirits – to dehumanize them. The Turks spread a dark shadow over the democratic society the Greeks had created, and that darkness could be felt in the hearts of all the Greeks that day as they listened to the Disdar speak.

"I ask you again, *Baker*. Why do you believe you have the right to sacrifice the lives of all these good people?" the Disdar demanded as he raised his right arm and gestured to the crowd of Greeks – who were now deathly silent. "Are you their new leader, their *Prokriti*…are you their god?" he demanded.

Elefterios knew that this was not a question the Disdar wanted him to answer. No. He knew that this was not a dialogue or even a trial, it was a sentence and he had already been found guilty. He resigned himself to the fact that his punishment would soon be dispensed.

"No, Baker, I reject your attempt to have these fine villagers punished for *your* arrogance and disrespect. *They* do not deserve the punishment *you* are going to receive. *They* comply with the law, *they* respect their Turkish masters, *they* will be allowed to live...." His words swept over the crowd, and a wave of relief seemed to reverberate from every wall in town. They were happy they would be spared, but shocked that Elefterios would not be.

Irini moaned and cried out "No, no!" Father Germanos and Manoli held her up as her legs gave way to her anguish and despair. Elefterios exhaled and stood tall.

The Disdar's guard suddenly dragged Elefterios closer to the olive tree and pushed his face into the trunk. With his right hand the guard grabbed the collar of Elefterios' shirt and pulled downward in a powerful motion, ripping the garment to pieces and throwing Elefterios partially to the ground. He then swung the rope-chain around Eleferios and the trunk of the olive tree several times until there was no extra cord hanging. He knotted the end quickly and then stood back as the second guard unraveled his whip and crept forward.

The first 'crack' in the air seemed almost unreal, almost as if it did not happen. The area was so quiet now that one could almost hear the leather tassels tied with bone chips and tiny pieces of iron swirling through the air before impact. The powerful snapping noise of it on Elefterios' unprotected back made the hearts of all the Greeks sink. Irini fell completely to the ground as she called out to the universe, "No, no, please!"

There was a pause from the Turks as they waited for either a howl of pain from Elefterios to come or for the blood to start pouring out of his new wound. They watched him intently as he clenched his teeth and closed his eyes, but otherwise remained immobile. A few seconds later, the flesh on his back bubbled and broke, and a dark crimson flow began to pour down his back. The Turkish guards cheered, and the Disdar smiled in satisfaction.

The second stroke hit his right shoulder blade – but Elefterios again bore the pain in silence.

The third hit his left kidney – a blow that immediately caused him to buckle.

The fourth struck him in exactly the same spot as the first. Involuntarily, Elefterios groaned in pain. His head dropped onto the tree trunk. He was being held up at this point only by the heavy rope that bound him to the tree.

Irini was crying uncontrollably. Father Germanos, Manoli and Michali were all overwhelmed with fear and disgust, but each felt helpless to do anything. The Greek crowd stood absolutely silent and most turned their heads from the scene, unable to watch the horror unfold. The Turks continued to cheer on the torturer; encouraging him to strike harder and harder.

The fifth, sixth, seventh, and eighth blows came rapidly one after the next. Elefterios' body was now covered in blood, and his flesh was peeling off his back in great slashes, separating his skin from his bones and making it seem as if a simple pull of any section would skin him alive. The ninth shot struck him in the temple of his head after which he instantly fell unconscious.

The roars of approval from the Turks were only stopped by the Disdar who, with concern on his face, approached the prisoner to examine him. After a moment of inspection, he signaled a guard to cut him down from the tree, at which point his body limply fell to the ground. The Disdar turned to the crowd and spoke in a harsh and foreboding tone.

"Let this be a sign of my mercy and of my strength. I spare him his life *today* and warn you all of your fate should you ever dare even think of challenging your masters again." At this, even Irini stopped crying, and stared at the young man surrounded by his guards. Turning to her, the Disdar then spoke. "Take him woman. He doesn't have long now."

He then turned and smiled to himself as he walked away in excited bounces, almost as if he were skipping like a child. A team of horses was quickly brought forth, and the Disdar mounted with his guards. In equal time the Jannisaries mounted their horses and followed closely behind. Then the entire procession of Turkish authorities began their march out of the village.

Irini and Manoli raced to Elefterios with Father Germanos limping alongside. Irini cried in great bellows of horror as she cradled her husband's bleeding head and butchered body. Relieved and shocked at the same time, they were all desperate to cover his wounds and transport him home. Half of the villagers stayed to watch them care for the man and the other half returned home in silence. No one noticed the tear fall from the eye of the last Jannisary guard as he rode away.

FOURTEEN

It was a full three days before Elefterios was able to sit upright in bed. As the rooster's call woke him, he stretched his arms and legs as shots of pain reminding him of his latest ordeal. He slowly pushed himself up onto his elbows and cleared his throat. He then reached for a glass of water at his bedside. At this movement, Irini awakened from the chair at his side and grabbed the glass before he could.

"Good morning, my dear," she called as her eyes met his.

Elefterios smiled as he leaned his head forward to sip the water she had brought to his lips. After a long swallow, he smiled at her deeply and with great strain pushed himself up to a full sitting-up position. The amount of pain he felt in his back at every small movement was incredible. In spite of how well bonded together he was, he felt as if his back had been removed from his spine, as it if were no long connected to the bones. The pain was excruciating.

"Good morning," he replied as his face cringed from the pain of the movement.

The room was full of the sweet smell of burning gum and spices that streamed from the brass chalice under the holy icons. A single brick of charcoal burned the incense and thin wisps of smoke filled the room and his senses. The nightmares he had experienced each night as his subconscious relived the torture he had endured, were somehow calmed by the familiar fragrance of the burning incense. It was that distinct smell that transported him from the bloody hands of his tormentors to the candle lit church where he and family had sat and listened to the service and prayed to God. It was a battle his spirit was fighting, and one that both his conscious and subconscious minds knew was not over yet.

Irini had kept constant vigil over her husband and watched his body writhe and struggle as he slept. She could feel the pain his mind and body were enduring, and she cared for him as best she could. She had tended to his wounds, feeding and caring for him, holding his hand and doting over him, giving him her complete attention, as only a devoted spouse could do.

His daughter was permitted to enter his room with her grandmother, but only when his body was completely covered and no blood or wounds were visible. Little Anastasia was in a constant state of shock at her father's condition. She was confused and scared by the brutal beatings he now seemed to regularly receive from the Turks. She simply did not understand why a good man, like her father, was beaten so. She was afraid to touch or kiss him, but she did so when prompted by her grandmother, although only for a second. She was too scared to talk or even to pray aloud; she simply watched and waited.

Father Germanos regularly came to bless Elefterios and to inquire about his physical condition. Other than Father Germanos, none of the other men entered the bedroom, each more comfortable with the role of guardian rather than healer. Elefterios' brothers, Manolis and Alexi, seemed to have turned into his personal guards as they sat in front of the house, silently watching all who approached. Papou Andoni , Gregori, Yianni, and Georgios formed a patrol around the immediate houses, reporting to Manolis and Alexi via whistles and owl hoots. The Greeks of the village came in waves, and control was necessary to keep their visits as quiet as possible so as not to alert the Turks of their activities. But the Turks knew. The Turks were watching.

In the bedroom of the house where Elefterios slept, the only two icons that the family had, those of Christ and of the Virgin Mary, had recently been joined by dozens of others that had been given to them after the assault. Over the last two days a steady stream of Greeks had quietly passed by their house in scheduled intervals supervised by Manolis and the men. The villagers gave gifts of everything from food to herbs and medicine, and sacred icons.

St. George the Dragonslayer was the most popular icon gifted. There were at least a dozen icons of various sizes of St. George in the room now, most with him riding his great horse, spear in hand, piercing the neck of the venomous dragon and saving the villagers from evil. That these were the icons being given to him, he knew, was no accident. In spite of his desperate state, Elefterios was conscious enough to hear several exchanges in the adjacent kitchen over the past two days. He knew what the village was talking about. He caught glimpses of Manolis, Alexi, Papou Andoni, Gregori, Yianni and Georgios patrolling the area and he understood what was transpiring.

He had heard Irini and Yia-yia Anastasia thank dozens of people for their gifts and their prayers. He heard praise of his strength, his fearlessness, his integrity and his wisdom. He heard old women cry and young men declare their loyalty to him. He heard their blessings as they departed, and he felt their love and support.

In those two days, Elefterios heard the word that had not been uttered by the Greeks of Ateni Samjak for hundreds of years. A word that had almost lost all meaning to them: "hope."

St. George stared back at him from all angles and Elefterios knew that his actions had created an expectation that he would slay the Turkish dragon, an expectation that he would lead them out of their slavery. The thought of it all was overwhelming and he dropped his head from the gallery of icons on the wall and closed his eyes to breathe in silence.

After a few moments, he opened his eyes and for the first time noticed a small icon painted in rich bright colors of Jesus riding a white mule into Jerusalem. A golden halo surrounded His head as He looked upon His disciples, led by Peter, following Him in to the sacred City. His right arm was slightly outstretched as He blessed the people coming out from Jerusalem to greet Him. The people, in return, bowed reverently at His approach. It was an image evoking a sense of harmony and peace. An image demonstrating both the dignity and strength that a man can show even when facing his own certain torture and death.

Elefterios struggled to take a deep breath despite the tightly wound bandages around his upper body that limited his ability to do so. He was reminded then of the physical pain he had endured so far and knew that there would be more to come.

Elefterios continued to study the icon of Christ for several long minutes. He knew that he could not meet the expectations that the Greeks now had of him. He knew that he was not a warrior. He knew that he was not a king. He knew that he was not their savior. He was just a man who chose to look to the light in very dark time. A man who believed that he had the right to do so.

As he stared at the icon of Christ blessing the people who rallied behind him, he couldn't help but fast forwarding the story to when He was captured and taken to Pontius Pilate, the Roman Governor in Judea, for judgment. Images of Christ being captured, whipped, and beaten filled his mind's eye and made Elefterios shudder.

He understood that many people saw the similarity of his fate with that of Christ's. He knew why they were looking for him to lead them now. He also knew that he could not deceive them or allow them to make him into a false idol. He had to choose his words carefully.

He called to his wife, who appeared instantly at his side waiting for his instructions.

"Irini, ask the men to come in with you so that I can tell you all what's to come," he said in a steady tone.

Irini nodded her head, fearing what he was to reveal, and quickly exited the room. She retuned a few moments later with Manolis, Alexi, Papou Andoni, Gregori, Yianni, Georgios, and Father Germanos. In a gesture of respect to him, all of the men took their hats off as they entered the room. They each greeted him warmly and lightly touched his hand or shoulder as they entered. He looked at each of them intently, but without a word. The room was silent in anticipation of what he was to say. Irini lifted a glass of water to his lips, but he shook his head and grimly smiled at her as he spoke.

"They will come for me tomorrow and they will kill me," he said matter of factly. Irini cried out and dropped the water glass. The men all locked their jaws in anger.

"They will kill me, but I will leave this earth on my terms: as a free man in spirit, not as a slave. Tell all the villagers to meet at the town center at the break of dawn tomorrow morning so that I may speak out one last time."

At this, Elefterios reclined back in his bed and exhaled deeply. Irini grasped his hands and fell sobbing over him. The men simply nodded and left the room.

FIFTEEN

It was dawn, and the town center was packed with every man and woman in the village. The area was incredibly quiet in spite of all the people present. Only the wind and the rooster's call could be heard as Elefterios and his entourage entered the crowd.

There was one man who should not have been there: Elefterios' brother, Michali. The Janissary Guard and converted Turk, hid in the morning shadows amongst his former brother and sisters, feeling as if he both belonged and was an interloper at the same time. He was inconspicuous with his large hooded coat, and he stood silent with the others, quietly observing the events as they unfolded. He knew more Turks were on their way, as did Elefterios.

Elefterios softly released Irini's grip and kissed her once on each cheek, then on her lips as he approached the open space to speak. He stood tall and proud, in defiance of the visible wounds that covered him. His chin was held high, and he raised his arms slightly in greeting to them all as he began to speak. The pain shot through his back as he did so – he cringed, but continued.

"Nothing new will happen today that has not happened before. *My* fate is not unique.

For thousands of years the Turks have dreamed of destroying us Greeks... of annihilating every part of our essence and being -their goal being to cripple our bodies and minds. To extinguish our spirits. To destroy our pride. To take away all of our hopes and dreams. *To break us completely.*

They have taught us to live with our heads turned down, to stare at the dirt instead of looking to the stars. They tell us we are dogs... and slaves... and scum and they treat us as such. They tell us we have no rights and live only by the grace of their Sultan. They tell us we are empty and worthless. That we hold *nothing* of any truth or value in this universe.

They tell us that we have no intelligence, no spirituality, no culture, no merit or worth. The tell us we have no past or future. They tell us that we are here simply to provide for them. To work *their* fields, to shepherd *their* flocks, to make *their* cheese and, in my case, *their* bread. They tell us that we are nothing. And every action they take is meant to make *us* believe that what they say is true. They condition us to accept this life as our unchangeable fate. And for the man who dares think otherwise, he will suffer the same fate that is about to be delivered to me. The same fate that has been delivered to all those before me who believed that a right is not what someone gives you, but something that no one can take away from you!

I believe that we do have the right to live... as *free* people. I believe that we have the right to praise God and Christ and to nourish our minds and spirits as *free* people. I believe that we have the right to take pride in the achievements of our ancestors, such as their building of the glorious Parthenon. This is everything! We must remember the Golden Age of Greece, where the greatest achievements in philosophy, science, engineering, and the arts were ever realized. Where democracy was born and gifted to the world. A time when we were free."

Michali cocked his head to the side and peered into the distance. He heard the heavy gallop of horses approaching from the north and he knew the Jannisaries were on their way to end this scene. As the sounds became clear to Elefterios and the villagers, they were again filled with fear and their hearts were sent to panic.

With no sense of urgency in his voice, Elefterios raised his hands to quiet them and continue. His voice remained loud and calm.

"Do not fear, my brothers and sisters. Remember that our forefathers battled the Barbarians to preserve our achievements and way of life. Remember that our forefathers *defeated* the Persian/Turk/Barbarians in the great battles of Marathon, Salamis and Thermopylae. Remember and take pride in our history. Remember when Alexander the Great brought their god-kings to their knees and ruled the world.

Listen to my words now. We must never forget our history, because it is only by remembering where we once were, that we can understand where we must be again.

They can rename our greatest cities, but we will never forget that *Istanbul* was and always will be *Constantinople*.

They can *call* us dogs, but they cannot make us *believe* that we are dogs.

They can tell us we have no glorious history, but we can never allow ourselves to forget our past... or our culture... or the fact that we are the founders of Byzantium, we are the children of Byzantium, and *that* this is our inheritance! We are children of God, and we are great."

The sound of the cavalry began to drown out his voice as the Jannisaries neared. Elefterios knew his time was ending. He paused before delivering his last words.

"Nothing new will happen today that has not happened before. *My* fate is not unique and neither is *your* fate. It is our obligation to honor our ancestors and to reclaim our past glory. It is our obligation to preserve our history, our culture, our religion... our identity! And we must fight to do so! Fight for ourselves, for our children, and for our grandchildren.

But in the time we now find ourselves, under the devil's foot, we must fight first to achieve one thing and one thing only: *freedom.*"

At this the villagers began to applaud his words. The clap of their hands and calls of support filled the square. With whatever strength Elefterios had left in him, he screamed at the top of his lungs: "Greece will be free! Greece will be free! *You* will be free!"

The Greeks were wild in their celebration and enthusiasm. They threw their arms, hats and hearts up to the sky. They ignored the horses and the black-clad warriors who forced their way through the crowd to get to Elefterios.

Elefterios turned to his wife and kissed her deeply on the lips, hugging her tight. "Do not mourn too much for me, my love. I will always be with you. And when you close your eyes you will join me in paradise, because I will be waiting there for you. I will...."

Before he could finish his words or give his wife one last kiss, Elefterios was snatched up by the lead Jannisary guard and thrown across the back of his horse as if he were a rag doll. The Jannisary Corps. had formed a tight phalynx and expertly wedged their way through the crowd in seconds. One of their horses was momentarily empty, until Michali discarded his robe and leapt on top. He reached for Irini and threw her across the back of his horse as he took his place in line. A third guard did the same to Father Germanos as the group quickly broke through the crowd and rode straight to the Acropolis.

# # #

Irini and Father Germanos sat on bended knees as they watched Elefterios being dragged toward a noose that hung from the newly erected scaffolding that surrounded the Parthenon. The sun shone bright now and not a cloud was in the beautiful, blue sky.

Standing in the adjacent building under a shaded spot were the Disdar, the Voivode and a foreign man in a bright colored uniform laden with medals. "Was that Elgin?" Irini wondered to herself.

The Jannisary Corps. stood at attention with the Pasha at their side, not one of them showing any emotion whatsoever. Not even Michali.

Without any words Elefterios was lifted to the top of a fallen column, and the rope was brought tight around his neck, then strung tight by the pulley on the scaffolding.

Irini lost her breath as Elefterios was pushed. Tears blurred her vision as she watched his body swing from side to side, jerking in pain, until falling still.

SIXTEEN

It was a dark afternoon. Heavy showers and strong winds relentlessly pummeled the Athenian landscape.

"Papou?" the young boy asked his grandfather as he stared out of the window of the Parthenon Gallery on the top floor of the Acropolis Museum. His eyes were locked on the Parthenon in the distance.

"Yes, son?" the old man replied without taking his own eyes off the temple.

"What year did he die?" the boy asked.

"It was 1803."

"When did Greece get its freedom?"

"A few years after that. Not long after Elefterios' murder, the *filiki eteria* was created, a secret, 'friendly society' whose objective was to organize a revolution to secure Greece's freedom. And in 1821, it was *Bishop* Germanos who actually proclaimed the national uprising against the Turks, which officially began the Greek War of Independence."

"The same *Father* Germanos who was Elefterios' friend?" the boy asked.

"One and the same," the old man replied.

"So the *'Elgin Marbles'* that we saw in the Duveen Gallery in London were the same ones that Elgin and his men were tearing down from the Parthenon when they killed Elefterios?"

"Yes. And to tie up a few other loose strings up for you, let me tell you that Irini Politis was actually pregnant when Elefterios died. About seven months later she gave birth to a baby boy whom she named 'Konstantine Politis.'"

The boy turned quickly and faced his grandfather. "That's *my* name," he said challengingly.

"It is, indeed," he said with a smile. "That baby was your great, - great, grandfather."

The boy did not seemed shocked by this revelation. It was as if he already knew it was true. He nodded in agreement and turned his gaze back thoughtfully to the Parthenon in the distance.

"Now you can understand what our role here is, son. It is now your obligation to your ancestors to memorize this story, word for word, and pass it on. Your job, boy, is to make sure that our history is not forgotten," the old man said earnestly.

Konstantine turned to him with affection. "No, Papou," he said. "My job is to fight for the return of the Parthenon Sculptures."

Papou Andoni looked at the boy and thought to himself. "Maybe the time for stories is over. Maybe the time for action is finally here. Greece could use a hero right about now."

# #